I0596760

NO GENTLEMAN

NO GENTLEMAN

A Novel of Love, Lies and Violence in Post-World War II England

THE SECOND IN THE THORNTON TRILOGY

MARY CHRISTIAN PAYNE

Published by TCK Publishing
www.TCKPublishing.com

Sign up for the newsletter to get news, updates and new release info from Mary Christian Payne:
http://bit.ly/MaryChristianPayne

To J.R.P.
A Gentleman

1

Anne Whitfield grew up in the village of Whitfield Cove. The town was named for her ancestor Albert, the first Duke of Kenbridge. As the only daughter of Lord Adrian and Lady Caroline Whitfield, the present Duke and Duchess, she had enjoyed an exceptional way of life. She'd lived at the family's country home, Meadowlands, one of the most magnificent estates in England, and whatever Anne wished for had been hers. She cried for a pony at age five, and a pretty, little Shetland appeared in the stables. At eight she wanted a playhouse, and Lord Adrian built a replica of Meadowlands near the duck pond. At ten, after complaining that her nanny was too stern, a new lady was hired, younger, prettier. She didn't believe in discipline. On Anne's seventeenth birthday, she was given an Alfa Romeo 6C and, in the same year, she became engaged to the Honourable Sloan Thornton, son of Lord Rowan and Lady Celia Thornton. They were the Earl and Countess of Wexford, and lived at Highcroft Hall, in the hamlet named for their family, Thornton-on-Sea. Whitfield Cove and Thornton-on-Sea were villages separated by an old wooden bridge that crossed a marshy inlet. Inhabitants of the two towns considered them one entity.

Anne was a beautiful girl, with tumbling waves of chestnut hair, rose tinted cheeks, and long-lashed blue eyes. In spite of what was clearly an overindulgent childhood, she'd somehow managed to escape becoming a demanding, self-centered young lady. Blessed with a sweet personality, everyone thought her charming and kind. The world was Anne's oyster until she lost her fiancé, Sloan, to Elise Lisak, a beautiful French refugee he'd met during the war. After breaking their engagement, Sloan won Elise's heart, and they married in 1945.

Along with the first disappointment in Anne's life, she experienced a new emotion – rage. When Sloan rejected her, Anne's dark side emerged. She did everything she could to sabotage his and Elise's happiness. But, in the end, their love prevailed. Anne had no choice but to retreat to Meadowlands, dispirited and miserable, having lost all hope for a happy future. She felt wretchedly alone. Above all, her anger turned inward. She hated herself for behaving in such an immature way – lashing out at Sloan and shattering what had been a lifelong friendship.

Anne had seen one other suitor, after Sloan. His name was Elliott Woodbridge, and ironically, he had been Sloan's Best Man. She'd met him at Sloan and Elise's engagement party, which she'd never expected to attend, but they had sent an invitation. To save face, she'd gone. Elliott was quite taken with her, but after a few dates, Anne lost interest. She wasn't ready for any sort of romantic relationship.

So, when the summer of 1946 arrived, she was emerging from a pathetically unhappy winter, having been nearly isolated at her parents' estate, feeling hateful and unloved, since the previous December.

<hr>

When summer came, Anne began to feel restless. She started to think about a new direction for her life. Since she'd lived in Whitfield Cove since birth, the idea of moving to London suddenly became appealing. She was no longer a child. At twenty-three, it was time to be on her own. She wanted to spread her wings and find out what she was capable of accomplishing.

After more than one lengthy discussion with her parents, they finally agreed to the proposed move. First, of course, she'd have to find employment. The idea was a bit frightening for a young lady who'd never worked before. Anne wasn't certain she was qualified for any sort of job. She made list after list of the things she enjoyed, as well as personal traits she thought might be strengths. She was organized, well spoken, outgoing, bright, and poised. She loved animals, fashion, art, helping others, and writing. Would that combination be enough to secure a position in a business environment?

After extensive consideration, Anne sat down with her father and asked him to give her ideas about how to search for employment. She told him that when she'd thought it all through, she was certain she'd like work that involved fashion. Her father mentioned that he and Lady Caroline had met the President of Havilland's Department Store at a party within the past year. His name was Randall Gorman. Lord Whitfield thought it might be worthwhile for Anne to contact him, to see if Havilland's might be willing to speak with her about employment possibilities. He further said that it would be all right to use his name. Anne rang Havilland's and was put through to Mr. Gorman, after telling his secretary that she was Lord Adrian Whitfield's daughter. Mr. Gorman was very cordial. She explained that she was looking to relocate to London and was seeking employment. Then, she gave him a brief run-down of what she considered her qualifications. He told her that he would arrange an appointment with the Personnel Director, a Mr. Frank DeLuca. She was afraid to become too excited. Without any training or skills, Anne questioned whether she'd meet their requirements. Her sheltered past made her naïve where matters of this sort were concerned. Anne didn't have the faintest notion that being the daughter of a Duke practically guaranteed her the coveted interview. It was not the promise of a job, but it did allow for a foot in the door.

She took the train to London on a foggy, May morning, and met with Mr. DeLuca. He was quite an impressive man. Very good-looking, with dark hair and brown eyes, he made an instant impression on Anne. She certainly wasn't there to seek a personal relationship, but she did notice that he wasn't wearing a wedding ring. Not that all men did. He looked to be in his early thirties. Anne sat down in his office, and a question and answer session followed.

"So, tell me a bit about yourself, Lady Whitfield," he began.

"You needn't use my title. In fact, I'd rather you didn't. I don't want others to think I'm above them. I'd rather be known as just Anne Whitfield.

"All right, Anne. How do I come to have you in my office seeking employment?"

"I'm twenty-three years old, and it seems like the time has come for me to be on my own. I've lived in a small village since birth. I'd love to experience life in London. To be perfectly honest, I was engaged to be married, but last autumn those plans changed. I'd prefer to try working. I hope to be qualified for a job in a retail organisation such as Havilland's. I've never worked before, and I hope that isn't a detriment. I *have* been involved in a lot of volunteer work for numerous charities, where I've done quite a bit of public speaking. I'm very eager, loyal and dedicated. I also have excellent oral and written skills, am well-organised, and out-going. I've often been told that I have good taste in fashion and that I work well with others."

She stopped speaking, and waited to see what else he might ask her.

"Where do you see yourself in five years?"

It was a very difficult question. The truth was, she saw herself married, with children. But, if she said that, would he think she wasn't serious about working? Anne paused, considered the question for a moment, and decided she needed to be as honest as she could be.

"I suppose within five years I'll be married. That doesn't necessarily mean I wouldn't still be working, but I do hope to marry one day. I have to be truthful about that."

"Of course you do, Anne. I would have been surprised if you'd said anything else." He smiled. Obviously, he'd been testing her. "So, then, am I to understand that you have no plans for marriage in the immediate future. I'd like to think that if we invest in you, we'd have you with us for a time."

"There is no one in my life at the moment, nor do I anticipate that there will be. As I explained, I've only just been released from an engagement. It would be much too soon for me to think in that direction again."

Frank DeLuca was impressed. He had expected that Anne Whitfield would be a rather unlikable person. He wasn't fond of spoiled, titled ladies. When Randall Gorman had rung and told him he wanted Lady Anne to be interviewed, Frank wasn't too keen about it. But, she had turned his thinking upside down. The moment she walked into his office, he'd been stunned by her beauty. But, it was more than that. She had an engaging presence, and seemed to be genuine. He spent much longer talking to her than he'd intended and felt he'd known her for a long time, even though they were from different worlds.

After they'd talked at length, he gave her a complete tour of their operation, introducing her to several of the top executives. She lunched with a group of Merchandise Managers and, by day's end, Frank offered her the position of Fashion Coordinator for Havilland's. The title was a bit more prestigious than the job, but it was still a coup for a twenty-three year old girl with no prior work experience. She would be putting together fashion shows for charity organisations and women's teas – pulling together apparel to be worn, publicising events, and acting as the moderator. With her beauty, charm, social contacts, knowledge of upscale fashion, and lovely way of speaking, she was a good fit for the job. The wages weren't enormous but, with her father's help, she'd be able to live a comfortable life. Lord Adrian had already told her that he'd subsidise her salary so she could live in a good, safe neighbourhood.

Anne thanked Mr. DeLuca for all he'd done to help her.

"It was my pleasure, Anne. I'm certain you'll fit-in at the store. I know it's not fun to go through the end of an engagement, but perhaps you'll find that in the grand scheme, you'll experience things you never would have done. So, welcome aboard."

"Thank you so much," she answered. "No, it wasn't fun to see all of my plans changed so abruptly, "she continued. "The war changed a lot of things."

"Yes, it did. I was in the British Expeditionary Forces. I think I fought in every major battle. I was more than ready to get out of uniform and return to my job. I haven't married either, nor am I in any sort of meaningful relationship. "

Anne was somewhat surprised at the turn the conversation had taken. Was he simply being chatty, or was he flirting?

"You'll find that a move to London will have quite an impact on your social life," he added.

"I suppose it will. I haven't thought about my social life in quite some time."

"Well, perhaps that needs to change," he smiled.

He *was* openly flirting with her. She was in his office because of business, and hadn't thought of him in any other way. She tried changing the subject. "Your family must have been relieved that you returned from the war intact."

"Yes. Quite. However, I don't see much of them. In fact, we weren't in close contact during the war." He launched into an explanation about the fact that he wasn't from the aristocracy. His father was a coal miner in Newcastle upon Tyne, and everything he'd accomplished was due to his own determination and effort. He'd graduated from Newcastle University and gone to work at Havilland's, until the war began. He told her that he seldom saw his family. "I have so little in common with them, which sounds shameful, I know. We speak on the telephone. I might add that I underwrote that luxury for them, so we would be able to stay in contact. They don't have any interest in learning about my world. My Mum says that she and Dad wouldn't be comfortable around my friends."

Anne was astonished that he would speak so openly about his family. After all, he didn't even know her. Of course he was in Personnel, and part of his job was an ability to speak with strangers and make them comfortable. Still, Anne wasn't quite certain how she should react to his personal disclosures.

"I'm sorry they feel that way," she finally responded.

"Anne. You're an aristocrat. You know as well as I do that they really wouldn't be welcome in an upper-class environment. At best, people would be kind, because they're my parents, but it would be uncomfortable for everyone."

"Possibly. It just seems awfully sad. They have a successful son and aren't able to share in what he's accomplished."

"It's the way of the world. I try to see them occasionally. They'd rather see me on their turf. Believe me."

"Oh, I do," she answered. Frank's lack of a noble background didn't interest her in the least. She was inspired by self-made men. In spite of being members of the gentry, her parents also admired men like Mr. DeLuca. She'd been raised to treat all people as equals, a somewhat rare way of thinking in class-conscious Britain.

There was silence between them. Then he changed the subject.

"Where will you be living in London?"

"I haven't decided yet. My mother and I are going to begin a search, now that I've found a job."

"Unfortunately, your salary won't be substantial. I know you'll want an up-market flat."

"Yes, but my father has already said he intends to subsidise my salary. You can imagine that they're not about to let me live anywhere but the best." Anne laughed, in a wry manner.

"I can understand that. Naturally, they aren't going to let their daughter move to London and live in an unsafe neighbourhood."

"No. I'm grateful for their help. Perhaps, eventually, I'll climb the ladder, as you've done, and not need their assistance."

"It certainly could happen. You have a better start than I did, what with your heritage. Anyway, I'm awfully glad you've come aboard here at the store. You'll make a fine employee. Would I be too forward if I invited you to have dinner before you started working? Also, I'd like to introduce you to some other people who work here. It will make you more comfortable on your first day."

"Well, that's awfully kind. I'd enjoy dinner. I'll find out what my schedule is and ring you. Thank you, Mr. DeLuca."

"Please. Call me Frank. I'm glad we've met and am delighted to have met you. I hope I didn't offend you, speaking so openly about my family."

"No. Most people probably wouldn't do so, but really, there was nothing offensive about anything you said. You're a very open person."

"Actually, I'm not with everybody. You're just a very easy lady to know. Forgive me, if I became too personal." He stood, and walked over to the door with her. "It's truly has been nice meeting you."

"Thank you. You've been very kind. I'll look forward to seeing you soon. I'll ring you about dinner."

After Anne left his office, she hurried back to the railway station for the return trip to Whitfield Cove. Frank was on her mind, as she rode along in a taxi. He was a very attractive man. Among other things she'd learned was that he was English by birth, but had Italian ancestry. That explained his colouring. He stood about six feet, was well-built, and dressed impeccably. Anne liked his smile. The only thing that bothered her was his tendency to speak so readily about personal matters. It wasn't exactly inappropriate but most people she knew didn't tell others their entire background so quickly. On the other hand, it was refreshing to meet someone who was so open. She decided to take it as a sign of honesty. She arrived at the station just in time to catch her train. It had been an exciting day. She was discovering what a wonderful feeling it was to have her first, real job. The next step would be to find a place to live.

At the next juncture, Anne and her mother journeyed to London. Together they explored neighbourhoods.. Havilland's was located in Knightsbridge, in the Royal Borough of Chelsea, not far from the renowned Harrods's Department Store. Though not nearly so grand, Havilland's was a well-known, upscale fashion emporium, known for its fine service and exquisite goods. They catered exclusively to women, and then only to those who could afford the very best.

Since the store was located in Knightsbridge, Anne and Lady Caroline decided to concentrate their search in the District of Kensington, a lovely residential area just west of Knightsbridge. The proximity to Havilland's would make the location a reasonable distance to work. After much searching, they found a lovely flat in an old three story Victorian house on Gloucester Road, near Queen's Gate Gardens. It was just what Anne had pictured. It had a bedroom and bath, a small parlour, dining room, and kitchen. There were two flats per floor, so a total of six in the old home. Gloucester Road was a posh area, where young ladies with backgrounds similar to Anne's could be found. The flat was furnished, so they only had to add special touches to make it Anne's own. That was accomplished in short order. Anne was over-the -moon. Everything had fallen into place so nicely. After a lifetime in a small English village, she was entering an entirely different world. While it unnerved her a bit, she was more than ready to begin a new life. She and her mother drove to London, in two cars, the week before Anne was to start working and moved her into the flat on Gloucester Road. By the time Lady Caroline was ready to leave for her return to Whitfield Cove, Anne was well settled and the flat looked as if it had been lived-in for a long time.

After kissing her mother goodbye, Anne made a cup of tea. Then she sat down in the parlour, looking around with pride. It was strange to have her own place. After a few moments the phone rang. It was Frank, ringing to ask if she needed help, or if there was anything he could do for her. She declined his offer of assistance, but accepted his invitation to dine. They had quickly become friends during Anne's transition from village girl to urban working woman. She'd grown to like him, after several dinner dates and no longer felt that his openness was odd. Frank had introduced her to several people who worked at Havilland's, so she already had a few acquaintances.

Anne had some new, rather innovative ideas for her job as Fashion Coordinator. The position was a new one at Havilland's, so she had the opportunity to be creative. She'd decided the fashion shows should be more personalized. Instead of using professional models, she planned on selecting ordinary people for the runway. It wouldn't be difficult to find young, attractive, debutantes and aristocratic ladies, who'd love the opportunity to take part in a fashion show at Havilland's. She'd already discussed the idea with some of her new friends, and every one of them said that they'd be interested in participating. She was off to a good start. In every girl's heart there was a secret desire to strut down a runway, wearing an incredible, designer gown.

On Monday morning she reported for work, discovering a small, but nice, office waiting for her. There was paper stacked neatly on her desk, a drawer filled with sharpened pencils, an up-scale fountain pen, and a dozen roses. The latter was a gift from Frank. It was all delightful. The walls were covered with framed prints of fashionable ladies in pretty frocks. A calendar lay on the desk with various appointments already penciled into its small squares. Twice weekly she'd be going to executive training classes, where she would learn the wider picture of the retail trade. She noted that on that first day she'd be attending an orientation session in the afternoon.

She sat down in the leather desk chair, gazing about the room. It was hard to believe it was her office. Only a month before, she'd been living the life of a Duke's daughter in a charming, but somewhat dull, country village. Today, she had her own office, in a highly respected retail organisation, with a title and her name on the door. As she took a moment to reflect on the turn her life had taken, the telephone rang. Picking up the receiver, she answered, saying, "Anne Whitfield, Fashion Coordinator. May I help you?"

"Lady Whitfield, I want to welcome you to Havilland's. This is Randall Gorman"

Anne gulped. Mr. Gorman was the President. She'd met him during her interviews, and he'd been very approachable. Nonetheless, she was somewhat intimidated.

"Thank you, Sir. I'm very pleased to be here. Please call me Anne."

"Are you settling in, Anne?" he asked.

"Indeed I am, Sir. I adore my office. I see that I have an orientation scheduled for today."

"Yes. I'll see you then. I also wanted to tell you that a reporter from the *Times* will be stopping by at ten o'clock to interview you. Since this is a new position, we want the word to get out to as many people as possible, particularly organisations that might want to collaborate with you for fundraising events."

"I've noted it on my calendar. Thank you for giving me a head's-up."

"Also, Avery Banister, the football great, wants some of your time. Apparently, there's a big match coming up in August, between Wofford and The Bridgeton Rovers. It will be played at Stamford Bridge. Because it's the season opener, and the first match to be played since the beginning of the war, an enormous crowd is expected. A portion of the proceeds will be donated to the War Relief Fund. Mr. Banister wants to discuss the possibility of a pregame fashion show and drinks get-together, in our restaurant, on the evening before the match. It would be black tie, invitation only, and top drawer. Do you think you could organise something of the sort?"

"Yes, certainly. There's plenty of time. When would he like to see me?"

"He'll be giving you a ring. You can schedule an appointment at your convenience."

"I'll be happy to do that."

"Right, then. I'll ring off for now and look forward to seeing you this afternoon."

Anne thanked him again and said goodbye. She glanced at the clock. It was a few minutes after nine o'clock. She had time to prepare for her newspaper interview. She scratched out a few notes regarding what she wanted to say to the reporter. A few moments later, the phone rang again. This time it was Avery Banister. Everyone in England knew who he was, and most young ladies were wild for him. He was a retired English footballer. He was named one of the World's Greatest Living Players when he retired in 1939, upon entering the war as an RAF officer. He was in his thirties and still unmarried, although there were rumours about his seeing a well-known actress. Anne was excited about meeting him. He told her on the telephone about the season opening game that Randall Gorman had mentioned. He also repeated much of what Anne had been told about the idea of a fashion show. They set a time to meet on the next Monday.

Anne smiled to herself. She was off to a good start. She already had a show to plan and was ready for her *London Times* interview. She paid a visit to the powder room, combed her hair, and re-touched her lipstick. She liked the way she looked – pretty and fashionable, but also efficient. She wore a black suit with a crisp white blouse, the cuffs of which peeked from the suit sleeve. Her tumbling, chestnut waves were upswept, in keeping with the professional look.

At ten o'clock sharp, a young chap knocked on her door, announcing that he was the *Times* reporter. They spent forty-five minutes discussing her new position, and he photographed her sitting behind the desk. She was anxious to see the article when it was published. After the interview ended, she sought out the training room, where she would attend the orientation.

2

When she reached the Training Division, Anne ran smack- dab into Frank DeLuca. Apparently he was to be a part of the presentation about the inner workings of a large retail store. He embraced her warmly, welcoming her to Havilland's.

"I meant to call you all morning, but got tied up in a meeting. How's the first day going? You look spectacular."

"Thanks, Frank. It's going very well. I'm here for an orientation – one of the classes I'll be attending for executive training."

"Yes. I'll be handling a portion of it. Has everyone been treating you nicely?"

"Absolutely. I couldn't have expected more. Thank you so much for the lovely roses."

"You're more than welcome. Are you off to a good start?"

"Yes, I even have my first show scheduled – well, not actually scheduled, but on the horizon. Avery Banister, the famous soccer star, is coming in to talk to me about a fashion show, prior to the season opener. It's a charity event."

"Well, that's a coup. Avery Banister. There isn't anyone better known. Wait till he gets a look at you. I hope you know he has a reputation for being a first-class rounder."

"No, I didn't. To be honest, I scarcely knew who he was. Do you see how living in Whitfield Cove has held me back from knowing the really important things in life?" she laughed.

Frank joined in the enjoyment. "I'd be willing to bet there are more people in England who know his name than Churchill's. Especially young girls."

"I must be in for a treat. I've read a few things about him, of course, but I'd better brush up on my English football knowledge. I don't know a thing about the sport."

"Don't worry about that. I'm sure Avery will be only too happy to tell you everything you want to know."

"You sound as if he's a Don Juan. Should I be worried?"

"No, he'll be a perfect gentleman. But, I'd be surprised if he doesn't try to interest you in more than football."

"Really? I read somewhere that he's engaged, or at least serious, about some English cinema star."

"Anne, you really are naïve. Even if that were so, no relationship with another lady would keep him from trying to sweep you off your feet."

"No matter. Athletic types don't hold much interest for me."

"Ah ha. And what sort *does* hold your interest?" Frank teased.

She tapped him playfully on the shoulder. "That, Mr. DeLuca, is none of your business."

"All right. Don't say I didn't warn you about the great Avery Banister."

"Consider me warned," she called over her shoulder as she entered the training room.

Frank *had* warned her. But the moment Avery Banister walked into her office, she was knocked- for-six. The man was magnetic. She'd pictured a large, muscular sort, with a swaggering way about him, and perhaps a receding hairline. Nothing could have been further from the truth. He was large – that much was true. And he was muscular, but not overly so. His hair was thick, shiny, and the colour of toffee. It fell onto his forehead, giving him a boyish appearance. He had a charming smile and most unusual eyes. They were blue, but she'd never seen such a shade. They were nearly aquamarine. Nobody could have ignored those eyes. Dressed in an impeccable dark suit, a crisp white shirt, and a tie that matched his eyes, he was quite simply a knockout. No wonder every young girl in England was supposedly potty over him. Anne was amazed that he seemed so nice. She would have expected arrogance, but there didn't seem to be any.

He extended his hand when they met. She asked him to sit down across from her desk. She was glad something separated them. She felt like a teenager and hoped she didn't blush. Remembering the warning Frank had given, Anne was on guard, waiting for Avery Banister to give some indication that he was on the prowl. However he couldn't have been more proper, keeping the conversation strictly limited to the charity fashion show.

Anne concentrated on his ideas, adding some of her own. She wondered aloud if there might be wives, or players' girlfriends, who'd want to act as models for the event. Avery thought it a smashing idea. He immediately agreed that by putting such ladies onto the runway, a much larger crowd would be attracted. Every one of the amateur models would have friends who would want to see them strutting the catwalk.

By the time Avery left her office, Anne was comfortable with him. He hadn't said or done anything inappropriate. She was charmed by his manners, not to mention his appearance. They made plans to meet again the following week, and it was clear they'd be working together frequently, as plans for the event progressed. She looked forward to seeing more of him. Anne glanced at the clock and decided it would be a good time to do her own tour of the store, leisurely walking floor by floor, so she could become familiar with all of the departments. She chose to do it in stages, using escalators instead of the main lift.

The sixth floor contained all offices and no retail space. It was the floor where her office was located, in addition to the Administrative and Accounts departments, Staff Training, the Staff Office, Public Relations, Advertising and Display. At the end of a long hallway, Display had a workshop. Close to that was the Medical Centre where, during working hours, there was a doctor and nurse permanently on duty.

The Fifth floor was entered by way of another door of glass, through an archway, and past an exhibition of modern paintings. This level contained the Main Restaurant and the Tea Room, Ladies Hairdressing and the Rest Rooms. If she went the other way, she would encounter the Book Department and Shoppers' Bureau.

Anne continued on, descending another flight to the Fourth Floor which contained linens, fine china, silver and other gifts. Everything a woman might want for the well-appointed home was there. The next two floors were devoted solely to women and girls' fashions. There was a large area called The Oval Room. It specialized in very high-end, designer apparel. One could find Chanel, Worth, Mainbacher, Givenchy, Dior – all of the most prestigious names in fashion. Only the very wealthy shopped there. There were other departments on that floor too, all carrying women's apparel. Nothing was low-end, but there were some departments focusing on more moderate price lines. There were separate areas for sportswear, leisurewear, outerwear, lingerie, sleepwear, career clothing, and teenage apparel.

Finally, Anne came to the main floor. Women's shoes, accessories, cosmetics, and jewelry were there, as well as a very high-end shop called Auntie's Attic, filled with mouthwatering clothing for children. Lace, ruffles, ribbons, and bows dominated. A corner of that department had exquisite Christening dresses with matching bonnets. It was a well-known spot, where British women went to find the perfect gown to be handed down from generation to generation. There was also an area dedicated to infant's furniture and little-boy's wear.

After touring the store, Anne returned to her office with a better picture of the entire layout. Mostly her job would call for interaction with the fashion floors, but she made a mental note to include some of the breathtaking children's wear on some occasions. People loved to see little ones toddling down the runway.

The afternoon progressed at a slower pace. Before she knew it, it was time to lock her office door and leave. She felt as though she'd worked at Havilland's for a long time There was still so much to learn, but after only one day she felt capable of handling the tasks the job required.

The next morning when she arrived at the office there was a pretty, young lady sitting in the anteroom.

"Hello," Anne said, smiling. "Are you waiting for me?"

"Yes, Miss Whitfield. I've been sent from Personnel to be your secretary. Well, I suppose they mean to have you interview me to see if I'm satisfactory."

Anne had heard nothing about a secretary. She was a bit confused.

"Could you excuse me for just a moment Miss – Miss –?"

"Alex Woods," the girl smiled. She was young – probably not more than nineteen. But she had a very professional appearance, with an engaging smile. Neatly dressed, with dark hair smoothed into a twist, Alex wore only a bit of lipstick and perhaps a hint of cheek blush. Anne liked her at once.

"Miss Woods, I have a quick telephone call to make. Then, we'll sit down and chat. Would you excuse me while I tend to that?"

"Of course, Miss Whitfield. Take your time."

Anne hurried into her office, shut the door, and rang Frank in Personnel. When he answered, she asked about the young lady sitting in her outer office.

"Yes, Anne. She's meant to be your secretary. Didn't I tell you about her?"

"No, Frank. I didn't have the faintest idea I'd have a secretary. What are her duties supposed to be?"

"Whatever you want them to be. I'm sorry I didn't discuss this with you. I should have. Please forgive me. In a position such as yours, you definitely need someone to act as your secretary. There'll be a lot of typing – plans for events, letters, and so forth. Also, when you're actually coordinating a show, you'll need someone else to make certain all of the fashions have been pulled and properly organised Once you really get underway, which undoubtedly means the moment the newspaper story is run, your phone will start ringing off the hook. You can't spend your day answering inquiries. You'll need someone to do that. She'll organise which calls are important, which need to be returned promptly, and which can wait."

"Yes, of course. I don't know why I didn't think of this. No wonder you forgot to discuss it with me. When you go through all of the duties, it should have been obvious to me. I imagine you just assumed I'd be expecting someone to assist me."

"Well, yes. But I still should have mentioned it. Would you like me to tell Miss Woods that the interview has been cancelled for today?"

"No, Frank, why would you do that?"

"To give you a chance to organise your thoughts, and prepare to speak with her. I shouldn't have thrown her on you like this."

"No, that's perfectly all right. I wouldn't dream of making her return. I just wanted to make certain there wasn't some mistake before I told her to come into my office for a chat."

"No. No mistake. This young lady has outstanding credentials. She's attended a fashion merchandising school and has excellent secretarial skills. I thought she demonstrated a nice attitude and common sense. I can see the two of you getting along quite well."

"She sounds great, Frank. I'm going to sit down with her now. If I decide to engage her as my secretary, when does she start?"

"I'd think the sooner the better. You two can decide that. But leave all of the other details to me. After you've finished your chat, send her back to Personnel. We'll go over wages, benefits, hours, and the like. It's fine if you want to tell her you want her as a secretary before you send her back to me. If she isn't the person you want, simply thank her for her time, and send her to me."

"Wonderful, Frank. I'll ring you when she's on her way back to your office."

Hanging up the receiver, Anne asked Alex Woods to step into the office and be seated. A pleasant chat ensued. Anne was pleased with Alex's answers to all of her questions. They developed an instant rapport. It turned out that Alex was a bit older than she looked. Anne had thought about nineteen, but she was twenty-two. That explained why she had such wonderful credentials. She came from a small village in Cornwall and, like Anne, had decided it was time to move on to bigger things. As a result, she'd enrolled in The Fashion Merchandising School in London, and tacked that onto her already impressive secretarial credentials. When the interview was complete, there was no question in Anne's mind that Alex would make a wonderful co-worker. She told her as much, and Alex seemed thrilled.

"I think we'll make a lovely team, Alex. This will be a perfect place for you to begin a career in retailing. I wouldn't be surprised if you moved up the ladder into your own executive position."

"That's what I'm hoping. This job sounds so interesting. I couldn't have asked for anything better. I promise I won't disappoint you."

"I'm not worried about that," Anne smiled. "You need to report back to Personnel, and they'll go over all of the things you need to know about salary and so forth. If it works for you, I'd love you to begin the next Monday. That will give you time to get sorted. It's obvious the store needs to furnish the anteroom with a desk, typewriter, and any other necessary equipment. Do you think that will be all right?"

"Absolutely." Alex stood, and shook Anne's hand. "What shall I call you? Miss Whitfield? Lady Whitfield?"

"No, no. Please. Just Anne. I'll call you Alex, unless you prefer something more formal."

"Not at all. Thank you again, so much. I'll be here next Monday."

Alex left the office, beaming from ear to ear. Anne immediately rang Frank and told him to put her on the payroll. "She's a gem. I look forward to working with her. Thanks, Frank."

"I'm glad she worked out. I liked her, too. How about lunch today, Anne?" he asked,

"I'd love it. I'll meet you at the employee entrance at noon."

At the end of one week of working with Alex, Anne knew her instincts had been correct. She was outstanding in every way. Alex had excellent people skills and seemed to know how to handle anything that came up on short notice. In addition, her taste in fashion was top-drawer. As they began to work on planning the Football Charity Event, they poured over every frock and gown to be included in the show. Alex had a wonderful way of visualizing what an audience would like. The two began to meet frequently with Avery Banister, and he was happy with their suggestions. He gave names and contact numbers for each wife or girlfriend of the team members. Alex contacted them, and a luncheon was scheduled, so that Anne and Alex could meet them to present plans for the show. All of the ladies were as excited as little girls about taking part. Anne was glad, upon meeting them, that the vast majority were very attractive young ladies. They would show off the fashions to advantage. Most importantly, they were the genuine article, with a sampling of physical characteristics. They were short and tall; some were heavier in the hips; others were top-heavy; two were expecting babies; and only one was rail-thin. Anne knew from personal experience that many women found fashion shows dispiriting. Afterward, if a person went to try on a gown they'd loved on the runway, it would often look terrible on them. Anne was creating a new concept – a show to which every day, real women could relate.

When the article in *The Times* was published, Frank's prediction came true. The telephone never stopped ringing. Anne's calendar quickly filled with shows of every kind. There were big, splashy events, small intimate teas, and Holiday galas. It was obvious that the idea of a Fashion Coordinator, who oversaw this new way of publicizing Havilland's, was an enormous success. More articles appeared in other newspapers and periodicals, featuring Anne and her overnight triumph. She was a bit overwhelmed by all of the attention, but it didn't go to her head. She kept her nose to the grindstone, concentrating her energies upon making each event the best it could possibly be.

As time went by, Avery Banister began suggesting they meet over dinner to discuss the August show. It happened so casually, and slowly, that Anne forgot all about Frank's previous warnings. She liked Avery a lot. There was definite chemistry between them, and he was on Anne mind more and more. She wouldn't have argued if someone had suggested that she was beginning to have romantic feelings for him.

3

It seemed that Avery reciprocated her feelings. Once their dinner meetings became routine, almost daily telephone calls followed, and then outings to the theatre, opera, and symphony. Of course, none of the latter had a thing to do with business. He began to tell her how attractive she was. Because Anne knew Avery was not only a good-looking man, but also a heartthrob to thousands of ladies, she was cautious. She even asked him about articles she'd read referencing his romance with the ravishing film star. He laughed and told her that those sorts of things were reported all of the time. If he was seen even once with someone beautiful and famous, it showed up in a tabloid. He warned her to be prepared for a lot of publicity of the same sort. Sure enough, he was right. Many of the more salacious scandal sheets spotlighted their supposedly torrid romance. When that happened, Anne stopped paying attention to anything written about Avery's love life. If anyone else mentioned the possibility of another woman in his life, she laughed and said no one should believe anything they read about him.

By the time the August fashion show came round, there was no question they were a genuine item. But Anne kept her business life completely separate from any personal feelings she had for Avery. The Gala Show and Drinks Party was a huge success. Not only did the store gain massive publicity, but dozens of gowns were sold. Avery even purchased one of the more spectacular ones. It was the traditional design that every large fashion show ends with – an ethereal wedding gown. Layers and layers of silk taffeta, Alencon lace, and crushed silk blended to create a delicious confection. If the purchase of that gown wasn't an indication of his thoughts for the future, what could have been? Anne was perplexed. He'd never mentioned a word about marriage – seldom spoke of the future more than a week in advance. In fact his lack of conversation about what was in store for them bothered her. She'd grown quite serious about him. There was no comparison with her feelings for Sloan Thornton, whom she'd once planned on marrying. It was like night and day. She'd loved Sloan because she'd always known him, from childhood on. But never had there been the quickened heartbeat, the gnawing desire, or the need to be with him as often as possible. She realised now what the difference had been for Sloan, when he'd fallen so madly in love with Elise and broken his engagement with Anne. The plain truth was that Anne believed she was deeply in love with Avery.

Was Avery in love with her? It seemed like it, though he never used that word. He acted as if he couldn't get enough of her. Because of who he was, they weren't together a lot. He travelled frequently, making appearances on behalf of various sponsors and charities. But even when he was on the road, he telephoned daily and often sent flowers. Anne believed he'd been so overrun with fans for such a long time, he'd become extremely wary of saying or doing anything that might cause him difficulty. She felt, in her heart, that he was in love with her. When he did something like purchase a wedding gown, there couldn't be any other explanation. He must have been planning to propose.

Autumn came, and then winter. Anne was very busy at work. The vast majority of women's organisations resumed activity after a summer break. Fashion shows at Havilland's had become the number one means of fundraising among upscale organisations in London. Large corporations followed suit with holiday parties. Sometimes Anne had two shows scheduled for one day – afternoon and evening. Avery was equally busy during the football season, putting in appearances all over England. Anne hoped that after the madness of the holiday season ended, he'd propose, and she could plan a late spring or summer wedding. They spent Christmas together at

Meadowlands. It wasn't the first time she'd invited him to her parents' home. His own parents were deceased, and he seemed to enjoy the company of her mother and father. Lord Adrian and Lady Caroline liked him immensely, and there was no question that Lord Adrian would readily have given permission for him to marry Anne. She hoped for a proposal and a ring at Christmas, but none was forthcoming. Her birthday was in January, and she thought perhaps Avery would pop the question then. It came and went with an elegant dinner at a posh restaurant, but no mention of marriage.

Avery had a lovely flat in Nottinghill and often, when they had plans to meet after Anne or he finished work, they'd meet there. He'd even given her a key. One evening, when Avery had an appearance to make at a children's charity, that was their arrangement. They'd meet at his flat and, go to dinner from there.

Anne arrived at half past five. She slipped out of her coat and looked around the living area. It was a typical bachelor's flat, and Avery wasn't the best housekeeper. He had a cleaner, who came in two days a week, but in between visits, the flat deteriorated. Dishes were piled in the sink, and pieces of everything from scrap paper to unopened mail were strewn about. Since she didn't expect him for at least an hour, Anne decided to tidy up. She started with the kitchen and had it in proper order quickly. Then she went through the parlour, putting things into neat piles, and discarding items that were obviously not needed. She continued on to the bedroom, doing the same. Opening a drawer in the nightstand, next to the bed, where she intended to put a stack of articles Avery had snipped from the newspaper, she spied a stack of photos. Curiosity got the better of her. Anne picked them up and flipped through them. Most had been taken at various events he'd attended. There were countless pictures taken at soccer games. She was about to put them back into the drawer, when she came upon one that showed an attractive blonde lady, reclining on the sofa in Avery's parlour. She was dressed in a black leotard, and her pale locks fell over one shoulder. Flipping through the rest of the photos, she found more of a similar nature. Anne knew the sofa was very new, so the photos must have been taken recently.

Who was the girl? Obviously the pictures had been taken in his flat, so the girl knew him well. She looked young – younger than Anne, but not a child, probably about twenty. Simply by looking at the expression on her face, and her poses, it was clear that she and Avery were more than casual acquaintances. Anne felt her heart speed up, but she tried hard to keep control. She knew Avery didn't have a sister, or any other close female relative for that matter. Clearly this girl meant something to him. Anne sat down on the side of the bed, turning the situation over in her mind. Should she confront him with her find? Or should she put the beastly photos back in the drawer, acting as if she hadn't seen them? She wasn't certain she could do that. She didn't want him to think she'd been snooping, but it had to be obvious that she'd been in the process of straightening the flat. Anyone with common sense would realise she'd come upon the photos by accident. She decided to mention her find. There was probably an innocent explanation. She and Avery were close enough that there shouldn't be secrets.

She finished her cleanup and sat down in the living area. She was reading the newspaper when he came in. Putting the paper aside, she rose to greet him. He kissed her and shrugged out of his coat. He was such a handsome man. Anne truly loved him and had reached the point where she couldn't imagine a future without him. She hated the continual feeling that some sort of barrier existed between them. He was always very loving and sweet to her, but the relationship never moved to the point where they shared intimate thoughts and feelings.

He sat down next to her on the sofa, stretching out his long legs. "It's nice to be home. Let me catch my breath, then I'll change clothes and we can go somewhere for a nice, quiet dinner."

"That's fine, Avery. I'm in no great hurry. Did you have a hectic day?"

"Quite. I was at the team office most of the day. They had a large pile of new publicity photos. They wanted my autograph on them, to send out to people – mostly children – who write and ask for them."

"Ouch. I imagine you have writer's cramp."

"Yes, a bit. It sounds like a silly way to spend a day, doesn't it? Signing your name over and over on publicity photos."

Anne took a breath. "Avery, speaking of photos, I feel like I need to mention something. As you can see, while waiting for you, I did some tidying up around here."

"Yes, I noticed. Thanks awfully, Anne. I shouldn't have left such a mess."

"Oh, that was all right. It gave me something to do. But – well – when I was organising your bedroom, I went to put some clippings in the nightstand drawer and came across a whole heap of photos. I couldn't help but look at them. Avery, I'm a bit confused. I saw several pictures of a blonde young lady, wearing a leotard and lounging on your sofa. I suppose it's none of my business, but it surprised me. Who is she?"

Avery's face took on the look of a thundercloud. She'd never seen that expression before. "You're right, Anne. They're none of your business. I don't appreciate your coming in here and snooping about."

Anne was stunned. "Avery, there's no need to talk to me in that tone of voice. You know perfectly well I wasn't snooping. Look around. You can clearly see that I was doing something nice by organising this place. I would never dream of going through your drawers, trying to find private things."

"Yes, but that's what you did, isn't it? I don't like that, Anne."

"Avery, you're trying to change the subject. Instead of answering my question, you're using anger as a way to ignore it. I'm not stupid. Why can't you just answer a simple question? Who is the girl?"

"She's a friend. Must I give you a list of every person I know? You don't own me, Anne. I think you're getting a little too possessive."

"Possessive? I've never once questioned what you do in your personal life when I'm not with you. We've spent an enormous amount of time together in the past months. You've given me every reason to believe that you care for me a lot. My God, Avery, you even bought me a wedding gown at the August fashion show. Don't you think most people saw that gesture as one of serious commitment?"

"I thought you were different, Anne. I didn't think you were another woman angling for a wedding ring. I bought that gown because I thought it was attractive. It was a whim. Something I did on the spur of the moment. It seemed plausible that I might give it to someone as a gift, or allow you to use it in another show. Who knows? Simply because I bought it, doesn't mean I intended that *you'd* be wearing it in a wedding ceremony with *me*. This is exactly why I've been cautious about our relationship. Because you come from an aristocratic family, you think you can have anything you want. It was obvious the first time I visited your parents' home that they've never said *no* to you in your life. I suppose you thought all you had to do was crook your finger and I'd fall all over myself wanting to marry you."

"Avery, I cannot believe we're having this conversation. As we began to spend more time together, I grew to care for you immensely. You acted like you felt the same way. Now you're making it sound like I set my cap for you, and went about trying to coerce you into marriage. That's patently untrue. All I did was ask about a lady who appears in a photo taken at your flat. She's quite attractive, and the poses are a bit risqué. I don't see why it's a crime for me to wonder if there's someone else in your life."

"There are a lot of ladies in my life, Anne. Surely you didn't think you were the only one, did you? I'm afraid you've gone way overboard in your expectations. I think this relationship has reached its logical conclusion. I'd like you to leave."

Anne burst into tears. How could everything have changed in the blink of an eye?

"Why are you doing this, Avery? You know you've given me every reason to think you cared deeply for me. Now you're making it sound like I'm the only one who thought this was a serious relationship."

"I don't want to discuss this any longer, Anne. I asked you to leave. Please do so."

Anne stumbled to her feet, in a blur of tears. How *could* this be happening? It was ten times worse than the rejection she'd felt when Sloan Thornton broke their engagement, telling her he'd fallen in love with Elise. Avery was being downright cruel.

"All right, Avery. I'm going. Apparently, I never really knew you at all. If this is the way you truly are, I'm glad I found it out now." She shrugged into her coat, still brushing away tears with the back of her hand. "I hope I never see you again," she sobbed.

"Don't worry. If I can help it, you won't," he spit back. "Now get out."

4

Anne cried for days. She'd never once failed to appear at her office because of illness, or any other problem. But Avery's actions had wounded her to the core. She huddled in her flat, refusing to answer the telephone, scarcely eating. She did manage to ring Havilland's to tell them she was down with a flu bug and couldn't come to work. Thank God for Alex Woods. She kept things running smoothly in Anne's absence. Avery never tried to get in touch with her. She lay on her bed, going over their conversation again and again, never understanding what had happened. The only conclusion she could reach was that Avery had been looking for an excuse to end the relationship, and she'd handed it to him. If it hadn't been that, it would have been something else.

Then, just about the time she began to pull herself together, an article appeared on the social pages of the *Times*. The announcement was made of the engagement of Avery Banister to Sondra Stamper of Bristol. The accompanying photo showed the girl who'd appeared in the pictures she'd found in Avery's flat. Everything fell into place. Obviously he'd been seeing her for some time. From what was written in the engagement article, she couldn't have been more different from Anne. She was a trained nurse, and while Anne had no way of knowing her background, she knew what it was not. Her father didn't hold a title, and it sounded as though she was probably a nice, middle class girl.

Anne understood at once that Avery didn't want a wife who ranked above him socially. He was a great star and a national heartthrob. He had every intention of maintaining that role throughout his life. When she thought about it carefully, she remembered comments he'd made about strong belief that the man should be head of the household, and expectation that his wife would be subservient to him. Avery was used to being worshipped by thousands of adoring fans. He didn't want to share the spotlight with a spouse. Anne didn't see herself as someone who would have stolen the spotlight from Avery, but she wondered if he didn't see *her* that way. Whatever his motivation, it was abundantly clear that he'd played her for a fool. Avery had probably enjoyed going about London with a Vicountess on his arm. Anne knew he liked being mentioned in the press as the escort of Anne Whitfield, the new Fashion Coordinator at Havilland's. She was humiliated and ashamed. What Avery had done was heartless and unkind. Surely he'd known that announcing his engagement, before most people even knew he and Anne weren't seeing one another anymore, was a giant slap in the face. He must have planned it.

She managed to dry her eyes and put a smile on her pretty face. She'd survived losing Sloan Thornton, and she'd survive this. She made a vow to learn from the experience and to be wary of the next man who came along. She wasn't so foolish as to think there wouldn't be another one. But the idea of letting a man capture her heart again was distasteful. All she'd ever wanted was a husband, a home of her own, and children. What seemed so easy for other women continued to elude her. It was an even more remote dream now, since she'd lost all capacity to trust.

***

Upon her return to Havilland's, one of the first people eager to welcome her back was Frank. They'd remained friends during her relationship with Avery, and Frank had known about her deep feelings for the great footballer. They had continued to have dinner engagements when Avery was travelling, and she had confessed her feelings for the soccer hero. Frank could have said that he'd warned her, but was kind enough not to do so.

Her first day in the office was busy. She had stacks of requests for show scheduling. Several people wanted to see her. She was glad of the distraction, and Alex was a godsend. She knew all of the ins and outs of Anne's involvement with Avery Banister, so there were no secrets between them. Because Alex knew that Anne was muddling through with a broken heart, it was easier for her to cope with the myriad of challenges occurring daily in her busy job. Periodically, the two would close the door, have a cup of tea and talk about everything that had happened. Alex saw the entire situation for what it was, and she didn't hesitate to say so.

"Anne, you knew he was a scoundrel. For that matter, Frank DeLuca warned you about him. I can see why you went for him. What girl wouldn't have? But don't feel that it was your fault. It wasn't. I'll bet he's done this sort of thing with a lot of women before you came along."

"Right. I think so too. I just can't believe I was so naïve. What made me think I'd succeed, where so many others had failed? I'll never trust another man again, as long as I live. This is twice that I've been thrown to the side for someone else."

"Not all men are rogues. Honestly. I know some really nice fellows. The problem is, they don't have eyes like Avery Banister's. You'll meet someone kind and good, Anne. I'm certain of it. I've always believed a lady finds the love of her life when she's not looking. Bury yourself in your career. When you least expect it, some wonderful man will pop into your life."

"I wasn't looking when I met Avery. He just appeared and swept me off my feet."

"Avery is a rare sort. There aren't too many like him. I've made it a point to stay away from men who're surrounded by hero-worshippers."

"Right you are, there. The truth is that I realise now how very different Avery and I are. We would have been terribly unhappy together. He has to be the centre of attention, and will expect his wife to wait on him hand and foot. I can guarantee he wouldn't have wanted to play second fiddle to my career – or even to share me in any way. He wasn't right for me. I'd rather have a decent man, who'll be content with a normal life. But it still hurts."

"There, you see. With that attitude, I think you'll do quite well."

"Alex, we seldom talk about your romantic life. You never mention anyone. You're such a pretty girl. Surely you've had your share of admirers."

"Oh yes, of course. Just no one I've gone over-the-moon about. There have been a lot of nice chaps, but mostly chums. I'm still waiting for Mr. Right," she laughed.

"Well, we'll wait together. In the meantime, we have three fashion shows to pull together in the next two months, so neither one of us will have much time for crying over the past."

Anne worked doubly hard, and if a social event called for an escort, she asked Frank to be her partner. He was always happy to oblige. There was no question that he carried a torch for Anne, but it was also clear that he didn't believe he stood a chance with her. Anne liked him a lot, but there was no chemistry between them – at least not on her part. However, as time went on, she began to wonder if the wild passion she'd felt for Avery was really the foundation for a solid marriage. Perhaps friendship and respect were more important.

Out of the blue, she received a telephone call from her old flame, Elliott Woodbridge. She had already been down the road with Elliott, and though she liked him, she could only see friendship in the offing. However, friendship was welcome during her time of healing. Elliott had seen the story about Anne in the news and was ringing to congratulate her on the success she was enjoying. They met for lunch and, upon returning to the office, he met Alex. It was apparent immediately that whatever had been missing between Anne and Elliott was very much present between he and Alex. They could scarcely pull their eyes away from one another and, before he left, they'd arranged to have dinner.

"Well, that was quick work," Anne laughed.

"Anne, I'm astounded. The moment I saw him, I felt he was different. There's something about him that I find very appealing."

"Apparently Elliott feels the same way. He's a very nice chap, Alex. I like him a lot – as a friend only, so don't worry. He's a school friend of my former fiancé, Sloan Thornton. I think you two might get on splendidly. He's a perfect gentleman."

Anne turned twenty-five in January of 1947. Her birthday brought on another depression. She began to worry about whether she'd ever have a home of her own, or the children she'd always longed for. She felt so old. A great many of her childhood friends were already married and had children. During that period, Frank took her to dinner one night and, after several glasses of wine, she unburdened her soul. They'd just finished a nice meal and were enjoying an after-dinner drink. A charming young couple came into the restaurant and sat at a corner table. They had a small baby with them. Suddenly, when Anne saw them, tears welled in her eyes. Frank couldn't help but notice.

"Anne? What's wrong? Why are you weeping? Have I said something to offend you?"

"No, no, Frank, nothing like that. That darling baby over there reminded me of all that I'm missing in life. It's so strange the way life works, you know," she said, brushing a tear from her cheek. "All I really ever wanted was to be a wife and mother. Instead, I've become a successful career girl — something I never dreamed of. I enjoy my job, but it seems life is passing me by."

"Anne," Frank replied, reaching across the table and covering her hand with his own. "Life isn't passing you by. You're young and gorgeous, and the best years are ahead."

"When my mother was my age, she'd been married for eight years. I can't seem to get it right."

"Rubbish. That's all women did in your mother's time. It was the 'done' thing. There are other choices for women today. A lot of them are postponing marriage and children in favor of a career. I, for one, admire that. I can't imagine having been married at such a young age. There are so many things to do in life. The moment one gets married and starts a family, all other experiences get sidetracked."

"Do you really think so? I can't imagine anything I want more in life than to be settled with whomever it is I'm going to grow old with."

"Good Lord, Anne. You're spending entirely too much time thinking about growing old. One would think you're forty. Relax, and enjoy the here and now."

"I suppose you're right, Frank. It just seems like life stretches before me with no hope of my dreams being fulfilled."

"Anne, am I being terribly presumptuous if I ask you whether there's any chance you could care for me? It can't be a secret that from the first moment I saw you I was a goner. I have very deep feelings for you. I'd be more than ready to make your dreams come true."

"Frank, are you proposing to me?" Anne asked, astounded.

"I suppose I am, in a roundabout way. I'm just dancing round the subject, hoping I won't be rejected."

If he hadn't used that word, perhaps things might have turned out differently. But he did use it. *Rejected.* She knew the feeling, and the word conjured up the worst suffering imaginable. His comment made her think. Might it be better to marry someone who thought she hung the moon, rather than the other way around? She respected Frank and was definitely fond of him, perhaps even more than fond. She found him very attractive, bright, and witty. He was a gentleman, even though he'd not been born one. They shared an interest in the retail world and spent hours discussing topics of mutual significance. Had the answer to her future been in front of her nose all of the time?

"Gosh, Frank. I'm stunned," she answered. "Are you serious?"

"Completely," he replied. "I thought you'd dismiss the notion outright, and send me packing."

"I don't know why. You know I care for you. I have to be honest, Frank. I was wildly in love with Avery Banister. But now, I think it wasn't the sort of love that makes for lifelong commitment. I don't feel that way towards you. I hope I'm not being too blunt. I don't mean my remark in a negative way. What I feel for you is much more sensible. Could you marry me knowing my feelings?"

"Anne, I have enough love for the two of us. I believe that once we were married, you'd grow to love me more and more. You're everything I've ever dreamed of in a wife. I'd try to be everything you want in a husband."

"You do want children, don't you, Frank?"

"Of course, in time. I have goals, as you know. I've always been much disciplined in the planning of my life. That's how I've managed to get where I am. I want all of the things you want, in the proper order; marriage, a home, the certainty of a secure future, fulfillment of dreams, children. Yes, all of it."

Anne only heard the part about a home and children. "Then, Frank, I think the answer to your question is yes," she smiled.

Frank leaned across the table and kissed her deeply.

"My God! Anne, I love you. What an incredible night this has turned out to be. Let me pay the bill, and let's get out of here," he nearly shouted.

Anne laughed aloud. She suddenly felt that all was right in her world. She was absurdly happy.

"I love you too, Frank. I've been a simpleton. You were there in front of me all along. I wasn't looking in the right direction. Oh, I truly *am* happy. We have so much to talk about – so much to plan."

"Indeed we do. Things like an engagement ring, wedding plans, where to live – the list goes on."

Anne felt relief sweep over her. There would be no more waiting. Perhaps Frank wasn't the man she'd dreamed of, but she couldn't bear the idea of starting all over again, finding someone new and going through the agony that falling in love could bring. She knew Frank. He was successful, good-looking, kind, and a gentleman. They wanted the same things out of life. Many good marriages had been built on far less.

⚬⚬⚬

They decided on a short engagement. Both were ready to get on with their lives, and neither was a child. Frank bought her a lovely, two carat, diamond ring, set in a Florentine gold band. Her parents hosted an elegant engagement party for them at Meadowlands, and all of her friends from younger days were there to celebrate her happiness. Even Sloan Thornton and his wife, Elise, were invited. They came, and Anne felt as though the rift between them had begun to heal. Everyone seemed pleased for the newly engaged couple, although Anne knew that Alex had misgivings. When she'd told her about the impulsive engagement, Alex had scowled and turned her head back and forth.

"Anne, I'm sorry, but I think you're making a mistake. You're doing this on the rebound. You don't love Frank DeLuca and, to be honest, I don't totally trust him. He can be charming, but it's my own feeling that he's a climber."

"A climber?" questioned Anne.

"You know what I mean. A man who's looking to marry into the upper classe. He's done very well for himself. University education, good job. But there's only so far he can go, isn't there? A Duke's daughter would top it off."

"Oh, Alex, you're being unfair. Frank isn't like that. I don't think he cares a whit about my background. In fact, I've always thought he'd rather I came from far less. He's never been enamoured with nobility."

"All right, think what you will. I only wish you'd waited awhile. It's much too soon after Avery."

"Rubbish. Avery was the mistake. I see that now. Frank was the one I should have been with from the beginning."

Alex put her arms round Anne and hugged her.

"No matter. I don't want this to affect our friendship. I'll have to assume you know your own mind. I *do* think you and Frank will make an attractive couple."

So, by the time the engagement party came around, there were no more negative discussions between Alex and Anne. Whatever Alex felt, she kept to herself.

Frank and Anne set about looking for a place to live. His flat wasn't appropriate, since it was only one bedroom, and so was hers. They debated leasing versus buying and decided to buy, if they could find exactly what they wanted at the right price. Both of them preferred an older home. The problem was that older homes, in good neighbourhoods, were through the roof, and neither of them wanted to live down-market. Anne made it clear that she didn't want to ask her father for any financial help. Frank said he didn't see any reason to refuse such an offer, if it came their way.

Of course the Duke *did* offer to help. Anne was his only child, and he wasn't about to see her live anywhere that wasn't top- drawer. After numerous conversations, Anne gave in. She and Frank found a charming house in Kensington and invited her parents to look at it with them. The house was situated at St. Mary Abbot's Court. It was everything they'd imagined. Actually, it was far too large for the present, with four bedrooms and two baths, but their plan was to grow into it. It had been built in 1920 and, besides its lovely rooms, there was a garden at the rear. Naturally, the Duke and Duchess approved. In the blink of an eye, it was purchased and placed into Frank and Anne's names.

The wedding was set for June 10, 1947, in the chapel at Meadowlands. Anne's dream was finally coming true

5

During the buildup to the wedding, Anne was far too busy to think deeply about the gigantic step she was taking. Perhaps that was the purpose of a large wedding, with all of its pomp and splendour. There was so much planning that one didn't have time to consider the true meaning of the event. The entire affair was beginning to seem like a theatrical production, with Anne as its star.

Lady Caroline took over much of the preparation, since Anne was in London. She organised the floral arrangements with a local firm, arranged for a musical group to play for the reception and devised a menu with Josef Lisak, owner of *Chez Chloe*, the restaurant he'd opened in 1946. Josef was Sloan Thornton's brother-in-law, as well as Elise Thornton's brother. Sloan held a fifty-percent interest in the dining establishment. From the moment it opened to rave reviews, people had been known to travel from as far away as London to sample *Chez Chloe's* outstanding French cuisine. Thus, Josef was the only person Lady Caroline considered when it came to menu planning for the wedding dinner.

Anne *did* have input, but for the most part, she trusted her mother to plan appropriately. She conferred daily with Lady Caroline regarding colour schemes flower choices and the number of attendants. Anne ordered invitations, which was an easy task, since Havilland's was known to have one of the finest stationery departments in London. The wedding would be large – over two hundred people. That included friends of the Duke and Duchess and practically everyone in the villages of Whitfield Cove and Thornton-on-Sea.

There was quite a discussion about who Anne would choose for her attendants. Alex was a shoe-in for Maid of Honour, but otherwise the bride-to-be wasn't at all certain about who to select. She and Frank had decided on five attendants, bridesmaids and ushers, including his Best Man. He asked Randall Gorman to serve in that role, and the rest were pulled from ranks of co-workers at Havilland's. Anne was somewhat surprised that he didn't have any very close friends. He did have five brothers, but none were included. Frank explained that if he chose one, he'd have to choose all. "Anyway," he told her "to be perfectly honest, I don't think anyone in my family would know how to behave at a formal event. They wouldn't have the proper attire and, to be perfectly honest, their dining habits are atrocious. I'd be embarrassed, Anne."

Anne was dumbfounded at his being ashamed of his own family. She'd never met them, but assumed she would before the wedding. Somehow it didn't seem right not to include family on the most important day of one's life. But, it had to be his decision.

"Well, all right, I'll leave that decision to you. Frank, but we do need to plan a time for me to meet your mother and father. It will require a day, or a weekend. We could run up to Newcastle for a Friday through Sunday visit, or just go for a day- trip. What do you think?"

"I hadn't planned on any trip, Anne. I would really hate to put you through that. It would be grueling. Plus, I think it's entirely unnecessary. Since I graduated from university, they've scarcely seen me. I don't think you totally understand my relationship with them. As I've continued to refine myself, they've become less important in my life. I've told you before, I have nothing in common with them anymore. They're perfectly decent folk, but we live in different worlds. I'll drop them a note to tell them I'm getting married. In fact, I'll probably even enclose a picture of you. Of course, they'll be able to read all about it in the news. But there's absolutely no reason for a visit. They'd think it odd. They really don't understand anything about my current life."

"But, Frank. They're your parents. I can't imagine cutting parents out of one's life."

"That's because your father is a Duke, not a coal miner. My father's idea of a social event is playing darts and drinking pints at the local pub. I've moved beyond them. We don't argue, or have any difficulty with one another. I believe they understand completely why they don't play an active role in my life. They wouldn't fit in, Anne."

"Oh, Frank, how cruel. I don't care if they can't even read or write. They're your parents. I'll feel ghastly if I marry you without having met them."

"Really, Anne. Let's drop the subject. We're not going to Newcastle. And they aren't coming to Meadowlands for the wedding. Do you think I want all of your parents' noble friends staring at my family, wondering why you couldn't have done better?"

"No one I know would think that. If anyone did, I wouldn't want them as friends. But I won't argue anymore. I do, however, expect to meet them sometime – even if it's not until after we're married.

"We might arrange that at some future date. We'll see," Frank answered.

Anne didn't belabour the issue, but the conversation stayed in her mind. She couldn't imagine Frank being so cold that he'd cut his parents out of his life. She wondered if there was more to the story. Might they have been cruel to him? If so, that would better explain his feelings. Anne intended to explore the subject further, but it was obvious that Frank didn't want to discuss it then.

In the end, Anne selected four other ladies to participate in the wedding, besides Alex. Although she wouldn't have believed it the year before, she rang Elise Thornton asking if she'd agree to be an attendant. After the terrible way she'd treated Elise, inventing lies in the futile attempt to make Sloan come back to her, Anne wouldn't have been surprised if Elise had flatly refused. But Elise was known for her sweet gentleness and didn't know how to harbour a grudge. She sounded delighted when Anne called. One would have thought there'd never been any history between the two.

"Anne, you're such a dear to want to include me. Of course I'd love to be a part of your special day. What a nice gesture. Sloan will be so pleased."

Anne questioned whether Sloan *would* be pleased. If it weren't for Elise's kind nature, Anne suspected Sloan would never have spoken to her again. After all, she'd tried to ruin his life by causing a split between him and Elise. But knowing Sloan as she did, Anne also knew that he'd agree to anything his wife wanted. He absolutely adored Elise. Anne felt good that she'd thought to include Elise in the wedding. It was the final action necessary to permanently end any hard feelings that might still have lingered. Besides, Anne truly did like Elise. She was hopeful they might be able to resume what had once been a pleasant friendship. Two other friends from childhood rounded out her choices for attendants – one a sweet young lady she'd known since grammar school and another who was married and lived in Tunbridge Wells. And, of course, there was Chloe Thornton.

At long last, June was upon them. Anne took off work the final week before the wedding, returning to Whitfield Cove to complete preparations. She had one last fitting of her wedding gown, which had been purchased in the Havilland's Bridal Salon. Then the dress was driven by special courier to Meadowlands, where it was hung in a guest suite, protected by a clothing bag. Similar treatment was given to the attendant's gowns. Everyone would dress there and simply walk to the chapel, which was attached to the main house by a small cloister. The groomsmen all had their morning suits sent to Meadowlands, as well.

The wedding was like a fairytale. Anne couldn't have looked more breathtaking in her gown of ivory silk taffeta and antique lace, nipped at the waist, a la the latest Dior styles. It had long sleeves with billows of fabric falling to the floor, in what looked like a puffball of meringue. The train was five feet long, also trimmed in lace. Her veil was held in place by a diamond tiara belonging to Lady Caroline, and the bouquet was a loose, cascading waterfall comprised of yellow roses, lily of the valley, gardenias, white orchids, and freesia.

Her bridesmaid's gowns were a delicate shade of pale yellow, also taffeta and lace, and the ladies wore crowns of wildflowers in their hair. Each carried a small nosegay of yellow roses and white violets. Little Chloe Thornton, Elise's six year old daughter, carried a basket of rose petals, strewing them in front of Anne as she made her way down the aisle.

Anne felt a bit dazed as she tried to remember to smile, strolling happily while holding her father's arm. Frank was waiting at the altar, looking very handsome.

Just before the ceremony, however, Anne was stricken with a panic attack. She'd never experienced anything like it before. Suddenly it seemed she couldn't get her breath, and her hands trembled. A dreadful feeling of doom came over her. She wanted to turn and run. Her mother was standing next to her, straightening her veil. She noticed that Anne seemed out of sorts

"What's the matter, dear? Don't you feel well? Your face has lost all of its colour."

"I don't know, Mummy. I feel frightened. This is such an awfully big step, isn't it?"

"Just take a deep breath, Anne. What you're feeling is normal. You have pre-wedding jitters. Take slow breaths in and out. You'll be all right in a minute. I felt that way before I married your father. I expect all girls do. Think about where you'll be tomorrow, when all of the fuss is behind you."

Frank and Anne were flying to Italy in the morning. They'd be spending a quiet, peaceful two weeks in a villa by the sea, on the Amalfi Coast, near Positano. Her mother's reminder of the picturesque place where they'd be staying *did* help to calm her nerves. Anne wasn't the sort who was given to such anxious moments. Her mother was right. After a few deep breaths, she felt herself return to normal. She smiled.

"I'm all right now, Mummy. What an awful feeling. I hope that doesn't return. You don't think I'm making a mistake, do you?"

Lady Caroline laughed softly.

"No, Anne. I think Frank will make a fine husband. Your father was a little concerned in the beginning, because of the vast divide in your social backgrounds, but he's come to respect and admire Frank, just as I do. I think you'll be very happy together."

Anne smiled. "I know we will. I was just being silly."

She straightened a lock of hair that had fallen loose from her upsweep and touched cheeks with her mother. "Thank you for everything, Mummy. I'm ready to meet my husband at the altar."

Anne didn't have that feeling again until nearly a year later. There was no question about its cause the second time around.

6

They danced for hours at the splendid dinner and reception. It took place at Meadowlands, in the white and gold ballroom. Lady Caroline, Anne, and Frank received guests, while Lord Whitfield ambled among the visitors. The room was decorated lavishly, in the same colours as the wedding. Yellow and white roses were arranged in crystal vases at each table. They were also tucked away in every available nook and spilled from charming Grecian urns.

The wedding service had been at seven in the evening, and at ten o'clock Frank whispered into Anne's ear that it was time to leave. She picked up her long train and proceeded to the elevated area where the musicians were playing. From there, she threw her bouquet. Alex caught it, and there was a lot of cheerful ribbing of her date, Elliott Woodbridge. He and Alex had become a steady couple, and Anne sensed that there was another wedding in the offing.

From there, both Frank and Anne went to the bedroom level, where they changed into going away apparel. Anne emerged wearing an ivory linen coat and dress ensemble. A small, sweet hat adorned her head, with a yellow feather peeping out of the top. Frank wore a dark suit, white shirt, and yellow, paisley tie. Anne's heart did a somersault when she saw him. He was her husband. *Husband.* It was such a foreign word to her. She liked saying it.

Taking his hand, they moved back to the reception to say their last goodbyes. From there, they ran down the stairs to the waiting car, which would sweep them away to London and a night at the palatial Savoy Hotel. Then they'd travel to Heathrow, where they'd board an aeroplane to Naples. After that they would rent a car and drive to the Amalfi Coast, where a villa near the lovely village of Positano, awaited. It had been a perfect event, and the new Mr. and Mrs. DeLuca were as happy as they would ever be.

From their villa they were able to explore the entire Amalfi area, as well as the Isle of Capri and the ruins at Pompeii. It was absolute paradise. They slept late, went sightseeing, and prowled tiny shops for unexpected treasures. The only time Anne found herself the least bit put off had to do with Frank's treatment of a waiter, following a sumptuous dinner at the Hotel Santa Catarina, which was known for catering to the rich and famous. It had been a lovely evening, but when they made ready to leave, Frank left a pitiful sum as a gratuity. It was much less than ten percent, or even five. In fact, it was more on the order of one percent. Anne was astounded. She was aware that Frank knew better. His etiquette was of the highest standards. There was no doubt that he was aware of how much a person should leave as a gratuity in a fine restaurant. However, she wasn't about to say anything. She certainly didn't want to embarrass him. Italy being Italy, the waiter had no difficulty speaking his mind. Luckily, he spoke only Italian. But, he managed to get across to Frank that the pittance had insulted him. Frank responded with a rude comment, and they left.

Neither spoke until they were back in their car, and then Frank broke the silence.

"Damned money grubber. I let him know all right."

"Frank! How can you be so nasty? I thought the service was excellent. Why did you feel he deserved such a small amount?"

"Anne. You may be a Duke's daughter, but I know something about the ways of the world. Why should I leave him any of my hard-earned money? He gets paid a wage. I'll never see him again. It isn't as though we were in England and might come back again and again."

"Well, yes, that's true. But – but – it's just good manners, Frank. It's the 'done' thing."

"Perhaps in your world it is, Anne, but not in mine. I work just as hard as that fellow. If he wants to earn more money, then he should go to university and get a good job, like I did."

"Darling, not everyone is capable of earning a university degree. Just think. We would live in a pretty strange world if everyone had an advanced degree. Who, then, would wait tables?"

"Anne. I really don't care. I'm not in the mood for one of your philosophical discussions on the plight of the poor. Let's just drop it."

Anne did drop it. But, inside she wasn't pleased with her husband's behaviour. She tried to imagine anyone else she knew acting as he had. Her father? Sloan Thornton? Even Avery Banister? No. Each would have done the proper thing. She felt humiliated by his behaviour. But, she wasn't going to ruin their lovely trip by carrying on about it. They'd be back in London soon enough, where he did things properly, if only for appearance's sake.

During the wedding trip, Anne discovered that she enjoyed the physical side of marriage. She hadn't known what to expect. Frank acted surprised that she'd never had a man before, but it obviously pleased him. He was quite deft at lovemaking, and she quickly got over any fear she'd had, since he made her feel special. By the time the weeks ended, and they were en route to the airport in Naples, Anne felt completely in love with Frank. She hadn't thought of Avery Banister one time, not in any sort of romantic way. She was very happy to be Mrs. Frank Deluca.

However, another unpleasant thing happened at the airport, when they were returning their rental vehicle. This time Anne was speechless. Frank drove the car into a parking space designated for returned rental cars. The next step should have been to go to the office and pay the bill. He had left a two day deposit, but they'd had the car for two weeks. Instead of turning toward the administration building, they boarded a bus which took them to the terminal.

"Frank! We haven't paid for the car. We can't just go off and leave like this."

"The keys are in it. They charge outrageous fees for rentals. I've done this before on business trips. Once we're back in England, there's nothing they can do. They'll just write it off."

"But, Frank. That's not right. We signed papers saying we'd pay the going rate. They could sue us."

"They could, but they won't. Do you know how much trouble it would be for a business in Italy to bring suit against citizens of England? It would cost more than the amount due on the car. It would be settled out of court anyway. People do this all of the time."

"I don't feel right about it at all. It's cheating. Can't we just pay what we owe?"

"No, Anne. There's no reason. You're used to having all the money in the world. I've learned how to stretch what I have. We're married now, and we're going to live by my rules. I know a lot more about finance than you do."

That was probably true, but Anne knew the difference between right and wrong. She said nothing more, but silently vowed to send a cheque to the car rental company immediately upon their return to England. Frank would never know.

She tried to concentrate upon the busy schedule facing them upon arrival back in England. They would have to be in their offices on Monday, which left only the weekend to move into their newly purchased home. Anne was excited about the move, but also a bit anxious about the work involved in combining two flats. There wouldn't be a lot of time. She knew they would be tired when it was over. The thought of aching from head to toe on the first day back at work, after two days of unpacking boxes and arranging furniture, wasn't thrilling.

Lady Caroline and Lord Adrian met them at Heathrow and took them into the city. Frank and Anne had taken their clothing to St. Mary Abbott's Court before their departure for Italy, so that's where they went. Their plan was to change into something appropriate for the moving chores, and then to meet the moving men at each of their respective flats. After the packing was complete there, they'd follow them back to the new address. Thus, they were surprised when, upon opening the door to the house, they discovered all of their furniture in place. Every painting had been hung, beds made, and dishes put up in the kitchen. Fresh flowers adorned every room, and even small knick-knacks had been arranged on various tables. Anne looked around and threw her hands to her chest in a gesture of genuine surprise.

"Oh, my gosh. How did all of this happen? I'm overjoyed." Turning to her parents, she exclaimed, "You did this, didn't you? This was incredibly thoughtful. You've saved us two days of hard work. Now we can relax and rest from the trip. We can't thank you enough."

Lady Caroline hugged her daughter. "It wasn't any problem. I had a lot of fun arranging everything. Of course, feel free to change whatever you wish. The important thing is that everything is here."

"It's perfect. Thank you so much." She turned to Frank. "Wasn't this splendid of my parents? Just think of the work they've saved us."

"Yes. Yes, indeed," he answered. "Splendid. Now we can eat our first meal in the new house tonight."

Anne thought it an odd answer, but perhaps he was a bit nervous. "Yes, but we'll have to have food. That means a trip to the grocer."

"No, Anne. Look in your refrigerator. We stocked it. I think you can get by until after your first week of work is over."

"Gosh. You thought of everything. Now, if I can only remember how to put a decent meal together, we're in fine shape."

"Anne, you're a wonderful cook. I couldn't scramble an egg when I married your father. I've seen you concoct gourmet meals."

"Thanks, Mummy. I do love to cook. I was only jesting when I said that. I'm excited about trying out new recipes in my beautiful new kitchen."

"Well, darling, eventually, you'll have a cook, of course. I can't imagine holding down a demanding job and coming home to all of the duties expected of a wife."

"No, Lady C. No cook No servants either. Anne is strong and healthy. I don't see any reason for us to spend good money on a staff. I can pitch in and help. I'm very neat anyway."

Lady C. was the name Frank used for Anne's mother. Her father was Lord A. Anne didn't particularly like the silly names, but it wasn't worth a fight.

Lady Caroline looked appalled. "No servants? In this big house? Frank, Anne will need help. It would really be too much, even if she weren't working. Anne isn't used to living that way."

"No, no, Mummy. It will be fine. I can manage. Frank is the head of our household, and if he feels that's the way we should operate, then we shall. We won't be here much, so the house won't get very untidy. Don't worry. We'll manage."

Both parents shook their heads and glanced at one another with looks of doubt, but the subject wasn't discussed further.

"Right," Lord Adrian said, "I think it's time we leave and let you two settle in. If we can do anything more, give us a ring. We're staying in London tonight, so we will be here until tomorrow morning. We'll be at The Ritz."

"Did you want to stay for dinner this evening?" Anne asked.

"No, not tonight, Anne. We'll come to dinner very soon, but you'll need to establish yourselves first. We'll speak to you tomorrow," answered Lord Adrian.

They exchanged hugs and handshakes, and her parents left. Anne was a bit unhappy with Frank's comment about not having help with the house, but she didn't want a row on their first night home. After all, he was tired and probably hadn't really thought much about their domestic arrangements. She went into the kitchen and began opening and closing drawers and cupboards, so she'd know where everything was situated.

"Wasn't it nice of my parents to have everything moved and arranged? That was so thoughtful," she murmured, as she continued exploring the kitchen.

"I'd rather have had the money," Frank replied.

Anne turned around. She was appalled at his statement. "Frank. It wasn't a question of money versus moving the furnishings. They were doing something considerate, so we wouldn't have to face such an ordeal when we returned. I can't believe you said that."

"It wouldn't have been very hard to move the furniture. It must have cost a pretty penny to have professional moving men do the whole thing."

"Frank. That's not the point. Now, please. Just be grateful for what they did. It was very generous and kindhearted. Not everything has to do with money."

"That's easy for you to say. You've always had it. If you hadn't, you'd understand what I'm saying. Ordinary people, who don't have titles, do things for themselves."

"Well, I'm not an ordinary person," she answered, rather flippantly. "And you aren't either, now that you're my husband. So, I suppose you'll just have to adjust."

Frank's attitude had angered Anne. She clearly understood that the difference in their upbringing was causing the rift, but she couldn't stay silent forever. On the other hand, she absolutely didn't feel like getting into a long discussion about how they were going to accommodate each other's points of view.

"Anne. I don't care for your tone of voice," he replied. "I know you're tired, so I'll let it go for now. But, I don't want to see any more of that attitude. Now, I think we should go to bed and get some rest."

"What, without dinner?"

"I'm not particularly hungry. If I am later, I'll forage around for something."

He didn't seem to care whether she was hungry or not. However, she acquiesced. Fatigue was undoubtedly causing both of them to feel cranky. Sleep was the best remedy.

But, sleep didn't come easily. Anne lay awake far into the night, tossing and turning. There were many questions flitting through her mind. Was she beginning to see a pattern of behaviour that she didn't care for? Back in Italy, with the waiter and the car Rental Company, and now with her parents' nice gesture, Frank seemed fixated on money. Was this going to be an ongoing problem? It hadn't been before they married, but they'd never lived or travelled together. Should they have discussed their views on money before marriage? They'd talked about it, but only a little. She'd made it clear that she didn't want financial assistance from her parents. She didn't mind if they wanted to present the couple with a gift, but she didn't want any regular contributions. Buying the house for them had been enough for a lifetime. Something like what they'd just done, surprising them with the move, was wonderful. But Anne fully expected that she and Frank would be independent from her father's wealth.

Frank hadn't argued her point of view. He *did* insist upon continuance of her career, and she had no difficulty accepting that. It hadn't been discussed, but she intended to quit working when they decided to have children. She couldn't imagine he'd have any problem with that. It had surprised her when he flatly refused to have any help in the house. Anne really didn't mind trying to do everything herself, but it was completely contrary to the way she'd been brought up. Every one of her married friends had at least one servant. Anne didn't mind cooking – in fact she liked it, but she'd never done much cleaning. Even when she'd had her own London flat, there was a girl who'd come in once weekly to do the deeper cleaning. Why hadn't they talked about it? She decided they'd discuss it the next day and, if she wanted a cleaner, she'd pay for it out of her own wages. Finally, she decided that these were minor issues. All married couples went through adjustment periods. She began to get sleepy. Turning over, she snuggled against Frank's body.

7

The next morning, Anne was up bright and early. She slipped into a pretty, silk robe and went to the kitchen. She planned on making eggs, sausages, broiled tomatoes and toast for breakfast, so she lined up all of the necessary cooking utensils. She set the table in the pretty breakfast room, using her best china and sterling silver and even wandered out to the garden picking a bouquet for the table. When she came back, Frank was up and dressed. She went to him and gave him a nice kiss, while reaching up and ruffling his hair.

"Good morning, darling. It's the first morning in our new house. I'm making breakfast for us. Just tell me when you're ready to eat."

"I'll grab something on the way to work," Frank replied.

"Frank, its Saturday. You don't have to work today. I thought we'd enjoy a leisurely breakfast and then walk through the house, deciding if we want to rearrange any of the furniture."

"No, since we ended up not having to move this weekend, I thought I'd grab the chance to go in to the office and get a head start on my mail. That way there won't be so much on Monday."

"Oh darling, do you have to? It's our first day together in our new house. Can't we just enjoy these two days before we go back to the rat race of the business world?"

"I won't be gone all day. We can have a nice afternoon together. Don't look sad. You'll find plenty to keep you busy till I get back."

"I know. It's just that I miss having you here, too. But, that's all right. I understand."

He gave her a kiss on the cheek and was gone. Anne put the pans back in the cupboard and made herself a piece of toast. She didn't feel like cooking a large breakfast for just herself. Instead, she went back up to the master bedroom, intending to go through boxes that sat on the floor waiting to be unpacked. They were from Frank's old flat. She wondered if she should get into his things, and momentarily stopped to ask herself if perhaps it would be better to let him unpack his own boxes. Her memory went back to the drawer she'd opened at Avery Banister's flat, and the terrible row that had ensued. She stood there a moment, trying to make up her mind, and then turned away. This time she wasn't taking any chances.

Instead, she went back to their bedroom. She wanted to organise a schedule, whereby she could take care of the majority of household tasks on weekends. She found she adored having a home to care for. With each item she dusted, Anne thought about who had given it to the young couple as a wedding gift. They had so many lovely things. She needed to begin writing 'thank you' notes too.

After straightening the living space and making the bed, she began to organise their clothing in the wardrobe. She arranged Frank's business suits by colour. Then, she found a rack and carefully placed each tie on it. Casual clothing and jumpers went into another area of the large wardrobe, pants on hangers and jumpers folded to put on a shelf. The bedroom suite also had an armoire that Anne designated as a place for Frank to keep pajamas, undershorts, and the like.

Her clothing came next. There was a bit of space left in the wardrobe, and she put seasonal dresses, skirts, suits and blouses there. A small cupboard in the corner held her underthings and sleep wear. Anne put her jumpers into a pile on the shelf, just as she had Frank's. The rest of her clothing, winter mostly, was placed into another wardrobe, in one of the guest rooms. She sat on the floor and sorted shoes. Finally, all were separated into his and hers, and they, too, were lined up neatly on the cupboard bottom. When finished, she was very pleased with her work and knew Frank would be, too. There was a small dresser in the same room, so she commandeered it as a place for leisure clothing, scarves, gloves and the like. She put her jewelry in the top drawer, lined with velvet, especially designed for that purpose.

Ann stopped and made herself a proper lunch of tea, toast and a soft boiled egg. She'd accomplished a lot. Next, she started writing the notes of appreciation. She'd finished over half of them, when her hand began to ache. So, she decided to leave the rest until later. Anne moved to the kitchen and foraged about in the refrigerator, trying to decide what to fix for dinner. That was an area where she really did shine. She wasn't terrific at plain, old everyday cooking, but she loved to try wonderful gourmet meals. Her mother had insisted that she take a cooking class when she was still in her teens, and now Anne was happy she'd done so. She knew Frank had a healthy appetite and would enjoy whatever she came up with.

At some point, whether he liked it or not, she intended to invite his parents, brothers, and sisters to dine with them at St. Mary Abbott's Court. It bothered her that she hadn't yet met them. It didn't seem proper. Perhaps that evening they'd have a discussion again about that topic. He'd said he didn't want to discuss it before they were married, but now Anne didn't intend to let it go. If they had poor table manners, she certainly didn't mean to allow such a trivial thing to keep her from a family dinner. There was no way she was going to be married to this man for the rest of her life and never meet his family. The whole thing was ludicrous, in her opinion.

Anne stopped working long enough to see if there was any mail. The post had always been a highlight of her day. Especially during the war, when letters from Sloan Thornton had kept her going. Now letters from her parents would be treasured. Really, receiving letters from anyone in her home village would be a treat. She missed her friends more than she'd imagined. Of course, she'd been in London for quite some time, but her trips back and forth to home had been frequent. Her parents had also visited often. Now that she had a husband, she wouldn't be as free as she once was, but letters were a wonderful way to keep abreast of everything happening in Thornton-on-Sea and Whitfield Cove.

She found just one envelope waiting for her in the postbox. It was from Elise. She sat down on the sofa in the living room, and using her letter opener, opened it. Elise began by thanking her for inclusion in the spectacular wedding and telling her again how absolutely top-drawer it had been. The letter couldn't have been nicer, or more sincere. A news clipping also fell out of the envelope. It was a write-up about Avery Banister's wedding, also telling about his having accepted a contract to play for some American team. Anne was quite pleased. She hadn't seen it, nor had she heard anything about it. She was happy to know Avery would be across the pond, so she didn't have to face the unpleasant prospect of running into him. She couldn't help but notice that Avery's bride was wearing the dress he'd purchased at the auction. The one Elise had thought was for her.

Elise went on to announce that she was pregnant. Tears welled in Anne's eyes. She couldn't help but feel that if things had stayed the same, it would have been her. But, she swallowed the lump in her throat and wiped the corners of her eyes. She was happy for Sloan and Elise. This was what he'd dreamed about. Hopefully they'd have a boy, so Highcroft Hall would remain in the Thornton family. A son would inherit everything, after Sloan's tenure. Of course, they had darling Chloe, Elise's daughter, whom Sloan had adopted, but a son and heir would be like frosting on the cake.

Unfortunately, because Anne was an only child, there was no male heir to take over if anything happened to Lord Adrian. Even if Anne and Frank had a child, it would not carry the Whitfield name, and could never inherit. The silly tradition irritated Anne. Instead, some distant relative would be the owner of *Meadowlands* someday. Her father had no brothers, so there weren't even any nephews. It would be some distant cousin she'd never known. There was still a remote possibility that Anne's parents might have a son — her mother wasn't ancient. She wondered if they ever thought about it.

She folded the note and put it into her desk drawer. After finishing all of her chores, she went back to the kitchen and flipped through recipes. She decided that since it was their first dinner in the new house, she'd make a fancy meal. She settled on filet mignon, wrapped en croute, with a sherry sauce. It sounded more difficult than it was, but tasted absolutely divine. She took out two filets and prepared the pastry dough. Rolling it on the counter, she seasoned the meat and wrapped the pastry round each filet, making neat, little packages. The steaks would be broiled in the oven just before they ate. She also made a lovely French sherry sauce to pour over the en croute steaks. Following that, she prepared tomatoes for baking, by cleaning out the insides, then filling them with a wonderful mixture of herbs, spices, and breadcrumbs. The only other dish was a rice pilaf, which could be prepared ahead of time.

When everything was ready for dinner, Anne decided to go upstairs and take a short lie-down. Climbing the stairway, she realised that she was still tired from the trip to Italy. She climbed on top of the four-poster bed and started reading a good book. Before finishing one chapter, she was sound asleep.

8

Frank came into the room while Anne was still asleep. It was about four o'clock in the afternoon. He leaned over the bed and kissed her cheek.

"Hey, pretty girl. I've found you sleeping on the job," he laughed.

She raised her tousled head and smiled.

"So you did. I worked around here nearly the whole day, and then I came upstairs to catch a few moments of rest and conked right out," Anne laughed.

"No problem, darling. What did you manage to accomplish while I was gone?"

"A lot. I cleaned the house, made the bed, straightened up, and prepared everything we're going to have for dinner, so it will be ready to pop into the oven when we're ready to eat. I also unpacked our luggage and put everything away. In addition I wrote a lot of thank you notes."

"That does sound like a busy day. I had one more thing I wanted you to do. I should have mentioned it before I left."

"What's that, Frank?" she asked.

"I need you to go through my suits. I need the inside of my trouser legs ironed, as well as the creases."

"Frank. I have to admit I'm no expert at ironing. To be honest, I've never done it before. Shouldn't you take them to a cleaning establishment to be pressed properly?"

"What? When I have a perfectly capable women here, who can do it?"

"But, Frank, I just told you, I'm afraid they wouldn't look very good. That's why they have dry-cleaning establishments. Surely they're not that expensive. My father sends all of his shirts and suits out to be done."

"Anne, your father is a Duke. I see no reason why I should spend perfectly good money on something you can do. So what, if you've not done it before? You can learn."

"But Frank, I don't know the first thing about ironing. I think I should hate it."

"I won't expect perfection the first time, but I know you'll be a quick learner. The major thing is that it takes time and steam ironing to get out the wrinkles. You have to make the crease set."

"All right," Anne murmured, feeling a bit put upon. She worked too, after all. Was she supposed to carry on all of the duties at home and also a full-load at work? When would she have a day off? Anne decided not to ask. She'd learned that Frank could be quite controlling at times. The best thing was to agree with him. She thought about dropping the trousers at the cleaners and picking them up on her way home. She left her home in the morning after Frank, and arrived home before he did. He'd never know. She knew she'd never get the pants to meet his standards, so she resolved to sneak them off to the cleaners and then sneak them back home again. Her assent pleased him. She wasn't as happy. It was ridiculous to resort to subterfuge over something so silly.

"That's my good wife. You'll get used to everything. You know, I have to get used to doing things I haven't done either. There are a million and one things around this house that need fixing."

"You mean you intend to do things like that yourself? Repairing cracks in the ceilings and the like?

"Anne, your upbringing is showing. Did you think I'd hire someone to do such chores? I saw my dad do those things all of my life. I'm quite good with tools. I rather enjoy that sort of work. Carpenters, plumbers, and such cost a bloody fortune."

"All right, Frank, as long as it isn't too taxing for you. I can't imagine, but if that's your cup of tea, get on with it." She smiled, and sat up in the bed. "How was your day at the store? Did you get much done?"

"Yes. I got my whole desk cleared. Now Monday will be a breeze."

"Perhaps I should go in tomorrow and do the same thing. I dread the first day back."

"No, that won't be necessary. I stopped by your office and Alex was there. She's been coming in every Saturday, while you've been gone, staying up-to-date. You don't have anything backed up, just a few details to sort out. You'll have to make decisions on scheduling some shows. So you can stay home and press my pants tomorrow."

Anne's heart plummeted. How in the world was she going to get out of pressing his bloody trousers? Then another thought came to mind.

"Frank. If you don't mind, I think I'll make a short trip down to see my parents tomorrow. Since I don't have to go into the office, it would be a good time to go. We saw little of each other after our return from Italy. They've been so wonderful. Would you mind?"

"Not if you find the time to get those trousers done for Monday morning."

"Oh, I definitely shall. I'll take them with me. While I'm chatting with Mummy, perhaps Vera, her laundry girl, can show me the best way to go about it. I think that's a perfect idea. Don't you?"

"Sounds fine to me. Don't be back too late though – I'll be wanting my dinner at the regular time."

"Oh, yes, of course. I'll decide what I'm going to make ahead of time, and have it ready to pop into the oven when I get home."

"Good planning, Anne. I think you're doing a very good job as a wife. I like your attitude. You seem to be able to plan a proper schedule so that everything falls into place. I like that in my employees."

"In your employees?" Anne was astounded. "Frank, since when did I become an employee? I thought I was your wife?"

"Anne, it was just a figure of speech. I spend so much time speaking with employees at Havilland's, reviewing their work and such, that I tend to speak in terms I use at the office."

"Well, I'd appreciate it if you'd try a bit harder not to speak to me like I work for you."

"The funny thing is, Anne, you *are* one of my employees. Oh, not at home, of course. But you are at the store. There's no need to get annoyed about it."

"I know, Frank. I just want to be treated like the woman you chose to love and marry."

"What do you think I intend on doing every night in our bedroom?"

"Frank, that isn't what I mean. I expect you'll be affectionate and considerate of me. That's what marriage should be. You know that."

"Anne, I'm not the sort of man who goes around kissing his wife in public, or holding her hand all of the time. Those things are reserved for private moments."

"You didn't feel that way before we married. But, I do agree. However, when we're alone together, I'd hope you'd find little ways to show me how much you love me. You did before we were married."

"Well, men do a lot of things before they're married that they don't do afterwards."

"I want our marriage to be good. I don't want to lose the love that brought us together in the first place. I'd like to think we might go out at least one night a week, just like we did before. I think that sort of thing keeps romance alive. It offers a chance for quiet time together."

"We'll see, Anne. What you're talking about costs a lot of money. Do you know what it costs to go out once a week?"

"Surely, Frank, with both of us working and earning nice salaries, not to mention my father's generosity in having bought this house for us, free and clear, we have enough to enjoy a night out once a week."

"I'm a saver, Anne. I should think you'd have learned that by now. I wasn't raised like you were. If I wanted something, I had to save for it. That's how I learned to be frugal."

"But, what are we saving for? I don't mean to be flippant. Of course we should save. Everyone should save. There are always unexpected things that pop up. I'm not at all one to go wild with money. My father was adamant about teaching me the value of a pound. But normally a couple our age would be saving for a house or a car – we have both - totally paid for. In fact, two cars, which is unheard of. I do think we should open a savings account and perhaps draw up a budget. That's only wise. Surely a dinner out once a week won't break us."

"Oh, Anne. There are many more things I want in life. We do have the house now, yes. But I want much nicer furnishings. In addition, I want a yacht, a wonderful trip through Europe and a home in the country, like your parents have."

"My Lord, Frank. Those are all nice goals, but we can't have them overnight. Those are way down the road. I've already said, I'm not opposed to a savings account. But things like yachts, continental tours and country houses certainly don't take precedence over other, more practical things, like children."

"To my way of thinking they do."

"What? But we discussed children, and you said you wanted them. You didn't say they came behind a long list of other things."

"I believe I did. I'm not at all ready to settle down to children yet. If I can't count on you to use some form of birth control, I'll have myself fixed."

"Frank! Over my dead body." Anne was truly upset now. "What in the world are you saying? Do you mean that if I became pregnant by accident, you wouldn't want it?"

"Precisely. I would expect you to have an operation, until I'm ready to have children."

"Oh my God." Anne covered her face with her hands. "You cannot be serious. What you're suggesting is illegal."

"You know very well that people from your walk of life can find a doctor who'll do it."

"Don't be daft. I married you because you told me you loved me, and I loved you. The point is, since we *are* married, and *do* plan on having children eventually, there's no reason not to start thinking about them before anything awful should happen to my father. My parents long for grandchildren."

"There's nothing wrong with your father's health is there? He's still a young man."

"He's fit as a fiddle, as far as I know. He's only forty-nine. There's every reason to believe he'll live to a ripe, old age. But, that doesn't mean he wouldn't love a grandchild."

"Rubbish. You're the one who's daft. We can take a few years to enjoy ourselves without starting to bring a bunch of little brats into the word."

"Frank, I'm astounded. Don't talk about children that way. I want babies terribly. I love them. Don't you?"

"To tell the truth, not particularly. In my family, every time another one came along, there was less for everyone else. Remember, I'm the eldest of nine. I don't see babies as a gift."

"Frank, I wish you'd told me these feelings before we married. If you don't really want children, you're not necessarily going to be the most wonderful father."

"Once I've done all of the things I want to do, I'll be ready for the little ankle biters."

"I cannot believe we're having this conversation."

"Just calm down, Anne. Perhaps I've gone a bit overboard in stating my feelings. But please, just give me time to rearrange my thinking. We've only just been married. Can't we take one life-altering thing at a time?"

"Of course. Perhaps I misunderstood you. I wasn't planning a child immediately either. I want time to adapt, just as much as you do."

They agreed to hold off on further discussion until a later date, when they'd both had time to cool off. They spent a quiet evening at home after dinner, and went to bed early. In the morning, after puttering about the house for a bit, Frank reminded her about his trousers.

"If you're going to visit your parents and get my trousers pressed, you'd better be on the road. I'll work around the house while you're gone."

He gave her a nice hug and kiss. Anne left the house carrying the suit trousers and walked to her car. Parts of their conversation from the night before still rang in her ears. She wondered if they shouldn't have spoken about the topic of children more deeply before marriage. It was obvious that the thought of babies didn't thrill him. Anne tried to be understanding. With the background he came from, it was easy to appreciate why he'd have such an attitude. She clearly got the picture. Now, all she could hope for was that Frank would settle down and realise that they were secure, money-wise. He needed to lose some of his evident concern about future security, and to lower his sights a bit when it came to dreams of country houses, yachts, and Grand Tours of Europe.

9

Anne arrived at Meadowlands about one o'clock in the afternoon. She' rang her parents from London, to tell them of her visit, and they were very pleased. Lady Caroline was waiting by the massive front entrance when the car pulled into the circular, gravelled, drive. Anne got out and gave her mother a giant hug.

"Hello, Mummy. I'm so glad to see you. We had so little time together while you were in London. I wanted to pop down and say thank you again for your thoughtfulness in helping us move."

"We were happy to do it, Anne. We had no idea we'd see you again so soon. I thought you two would be cosied up in your house, extending your wedding trip by a couple of days."

"Yes. Well, Frank, the ever-faithful employee, wanted to go into his office yesterday, so I worked on unpacking boxes and got everything in order. Today he's doing work around the house, so I decided to pay you a visit. Once I go back to work, there won't be a chance to come see you as often. I imagine we'll be busy on weekends. Plus, we never even had a chance to talk about the wedding and our wedding trip. So here I am."

"We're delighted you're here. So, are you enjoying married life? I know it's soon, but I hope you're very happy."

"Yes, I am. There are a few little kinks we have to work out. I think that's normal for any marriage, especially in the beginning. But for the most part, we're off to a good start."

"Anne, darling, it's a bit soon for little kinks. Is everything all right?"

"Yes, yes. I've just realised that Frank and I *do* come from very different backgrounds. Growing up poor affected him greatly. I have to learn to adapt to those parts of his personality that have been shaped by his upbringing."

"Such as . . . "

Anne turned and opened the rear car door. She reached in and collected the pile of suit pants. "Like expecting me to press his suit trousers for him, rather than sending them to a cleaning establishment."

"What? Press his trousers? Anne, do you even know how to iron?"

"Not really," she laughed. "But I'll learn. I told him I was bringing them on this visit so Vera could teach me how to do it. But, I really intend to ask Vera to do it for me, since I haven't much time to spend with you and don't want to waste it in the laundry room."

Vera was the maid who saw to washing, ironing and the like. Actually, even Vera wasn't all that familiar with pressing men's suit pants, since such things were sent out at the Whitfield estate. But, she'd be better at it than Anne.

"Anne. I'm astounded. Surely Frank can afford to have clothing dry cleaned."

"Well of course he can – I mean *we* can. It's apparent that he's of the belief that being married means the wife sees to those chores. It saves money. He's very close with a pound."

"Anne, you can't work all day and then do everything at home, too. His comment about you not having a maid to help with cleaning astounded me. What if your father and I were to pay?"

"No, Mummy. I'm married now. I've made it clear to Frank that you two aren't going to support us. I think what you did when you bought the house was unbelievable. It would have taken us years to be able to save enough money to buy such a splendid place. We're on our own. Other wives work and take care of the home. I can do it, too. Thank goodness I love to cook."

"Well, I have to be honest and tell you that I don't like it. I don't like it one bit. But I don't want to be an interfering mother-in-law. I'm sure you'll work it out," Lady Caroline said, as they walked into the house.

She immediately rang for Vera and explained about the pants. Even Vera raised an eyebrow. Anne couldn't help but laugh. Vera left the room, carrying the heap of trousers, saying she'd have them ready before Anne returned to London.

Mother and daughter settled in the drawing room, and rang for a tea tray. Soon after, Lord Adrian came home, following a meeting with his estate manager.

"Well, my dear Anne," he exclaimed. "I didn't think we'd be seeing you so soon. I'm glad you're here."

"I know. As I told Mummy, it was a good opportunity. I go back to work tomorrow and probably won't have the chance to visit for a while."

"She also had to bring Frank's trousers down from London to be pressed," Lady Caroline said sarcastically.

"His trousers? Surely you can't be serious?"

"Oh, indeed, I am," answered his wife. She went on to explain about why their daughter had arrived with several pairs of trousers. Lord Adrian was amazed.

"Anne, it's not my business to poke my nose into your affairs, but I hope you're not going to become one of those wives who lets her husband order her around. Of course, the man should be the head of the household. But there's a limit. You're the daughter of a Duke. He must know that you're not used to such tasks. It would be one thing if money were an issue – if you were living on a shoestring. First of all, I bought you the house, free and clear. Secondly, Frank was given a dowry. A very substantial, over six-figure dowry. Third, both of you hold responsible jobs. There is certainly no reason why you should be expected to press pants. 'E Gads!"

"I know, Father. I don't intend to be a slave, believe me. But Frank has to adjust. Just because I'm the daughter of a Duke, we have to remember that Frank doesn't come from nobility. He'll learn. He's always had to watch every bit of money he's had. It will take some loosening of restraints. Also, he still has some lofty goals."

"What sort of goals?" Lord Adrian asked.

"Oh, he wants to have a great house in the country someday, and a yacht, and a Grand Tour of the Continent."

"How old is Frank? In his early thirties, right?"

"Yes. Thirty-four," Anne answered.

"My dear daughter. You'll inherit a great deal of money at my passing. There isn't a necessity to start out with everything. Where in blazes is he going to put a yacht? In the Thames?"

"I don't know," Anne replied. "People do have watercraft. I suppose he thinks we'll have a second home on the water."

"And a Grand Tour? My God, Anne. He's just returned from the bloody war. Pardon my language, but this is a bit over-the-top. I'd think he'd seen enough of the continent for a while. All of those things can wait. If he wanted to do them, why did he get married? Most young men do the Grand Tour before they're ready to settle down."

"Yes. But, Father, Frank didn't have that opportunity. You know his family is very poor. His father is a coal miner. They couldn't have sent Frank on a tour of the Continent."

"Well, to be honest, I think he has some big ideas for one so young. I admire him for what he's accomplished, and I like the chap. But he needs to realise that he's very fortunate. He has a good life now. All of the things you mentioned can wait."

"I think he'll realise that, Father. We've only been married less than two weeks. My goodness. Let's allow him time. It's just that he's had to spend his life scrimping and saving to accomplish the things he has. It's a way of life for him. I'd rather have that than a terrible spendthrift. At least he isn't a gambler."

"That much is true, Adrian," added Lady Caroline. "We need to give the boy a chance."

"I suppose you're right. I simply don't like the idea of your pressing pants and God knows whatever else he expects."

Anne smiled and patted her father on the shoulder.

"I'm fine Father. Everything is going to work out splendidly. He's a good man, and we have a lot in common. Now, tell me about happenings in Whitfield Cove and Thornton-on-Sea."

———

Anne retuned home about six o'clock, with freshly ironed trousers draped over her arm. Frank was in one of the spare bedrooms, polishing the brass on a lovely bed they'd purchased for a song in an antique store. It was in dire need of polish, but Frank had insisted he could take care of that, and sure enough, it was shining like the sun. He must have been working on it all day.

She deposited the pants in his wardrobe and joined him.

"What a wonderful job you've done. You were right. It looks wonderful. That must have taken a good amount of elbow grease."

"Yes, it's been a task. But I like to do things like this. It's a reward to see something old and worn brought back to new. Not everyone has the money to pay someone to do these sort of tasks for them."

"I know that, Frank. I'm proud of the work you've done. It's beautiful."

He stood back, and stretched his arms above his shoulders.

"How was your visit?" he asked.

"Wonderful. Mummy and Father were glad to see me. They were sorry you couldn't have come, too."

"Did you get my pants pressed?"

"Yes, I did."

"So, you know how to do it now? I'll expect them to be done every week. There's no reason to send a suit out every time it's worn. The only thing it needs is a good pressing."

"Perhaps we should get a pants press. You know. Like they have in posh hotels. They're not terribly expensive, and you could just come home at night and hang them on that. They'd be perfect in nothing flat."

"Those things aren't cheap, Anne. Why in the world would we do that, when you can do it yourself?"

"What did you do before we were married?"

"I sent them out. But there's no need for that now."

Anne didn't say anything more. She didn't feel like getting into a row about his silly pants. Instead, she changed the subject to their dinner.

"Frank, since I've been gone most of the day, and you've worked hard on the bed, why don't we run out and grab a bite to eat? You know, just something simple. I'm rather fagged out and don't feel like cooking."

"Anne, if you're too tired to cook, you shouldn't have driven to Meadowlands and back. I was afraid of that. I'm awfully hungry, too. Surely you can whip something together?"

"I suppose I could, but I don't feel like it. I'm tired, Frank. If you don't want to come with me, fine. But, I'm going out to grab a quick meal."

"Without me?"

"I'd like you to come with me, but if you don't want to, then yes, I'll go alone."

"All right. I'll come, too. But we're not going to make a habit of this. From now on I expect you to plan better. You should have known what we were going to eat before leaving."

"Frank, I *did* have a plan for what I would fix. But, I didn't think I'd be so tired. Can we please just get on with it?"

Anne shook her head. Frank followed her down the stairs, and they walked to the kerb together. Anne still drove the car she'd been given on her eighteenth birthday. It scarcely had any miles on it, since she'd lived in such a small village. She loved it dearly, even though it was ten years old. Frank, on the other hand, drove a spanking new, canary yellow Ferrari 125 S. It had debuted in May, just before their wedding. He absolutely forbade her to drive it. Anne couldn't have cared less. While she thought he was a bit childish about the car, she understood he'd never had anything remotely like it, and it was like a splendid toy would be to a small boy. When they went out together, they always drove it, since Frank was behind the wheel.

They went to a mediocre bistro, near their home. He parked at the kerb, and they went inside to eat. An hour later they exited the restaurant to find that someone had sideswiped his gorgeous car. She'd never seen Frank in such a tirade. He swore and screamed and finally blamed it on Anne. If she hadn't insisted on going out to eat, it would never have happened. There was no point in arguing, as it was obvious that he would only become angrier. Frank insisted upon calling his insurance company from a phone booth, and it was an hour before he calmed down enough to drive home. He ranted all the way back to the house and stomped inside without waiting for her. Anne held back tears as she walked the pathway to the door. She felt like she was married to a child.

10

They returned to work the following day. It wasn't a pleasant morning. Although Anne cooked a lovely breakfast and tried to make small talk while they ate, Frank continued to sulk about his car. Ann knew better than to try to minimize the situation. In reality, there was very little for Frank to be pouting about. The car was badly scraped on one side, but the insurance adjuster had already been to visit. He predicted the automobile would be back within a week, and there would be no trace of the damage. However, Frank seemed hell bent on blaming his wife for what had happened. He apparently enjoyed pouting.

In any event, both of them climbed into Ann's car and drove to Havilland's. Anne knew all of their co-workers would be anxious to hear about the wedding trip, and it would look frightful if the happy couple turned up at work looking downcast and depressed. So she put a cheerful smile on her face and urged her husband to do the same. If Frank cared about anything, it was his job, so he complied. Anne was actually glad when they parted ways, each going to their own office. She knew Frank's secretary would probably have to listen all day to his lamentations about the tragedy. Anne was happy to see Alex's pretty face waiting in the anteroom, anxious to hear about Italy.

Anne's desk was stacked high with numerous requests and invitations to business social gatherings. It was nearly July, and new trends for autumn would be arriving in the store before long. It seemed like everyone loved the idea of a fashion show to celebrate back-to-school time. She sorted through the mail, making two stacks – one to throw in the bin and another requiring an answer, or action of some kind. In all, it looked like she would be coordinating four shows in September and at least two in October. Of course the Holidays would also be upon them soon. She would be deluged with requests for Christmas galas. It felt good to be back at the store. She felt in command in her own little office, not having to worry about whether she was pleasing her husband. She hoped their present difficulties would be resolved soon. She and Frank shouldn't have been arguing such a short time after the wedding. She kept telling herself that it was all connected to the early marriage jitters, along with getting to know one another better. "This too shall pass," she kept repeating to herself.

Anne didn't want to tell Alex about the problems that had popped up. After all, Alex was the one who'd told her she was making a mistake. While she said nothing about the fight with Frank, she couldn't help but think back over some of the things Alex had warned her about. Especially the part about how Frank was a *climber*. She remembered his comment about how he'd rather have had the money than her parents' kind gesture in moving their furniture to the new house. Money was definitely a huge issue with her husband. He liked it immensely, but he certainly didn't want to spend any of it. Again, she remembered the embarrassing moment with the waiter at the Santa Catarina Hotel, as well as the rental car fiasco. Anne *had* posted a cheque to them immediately upon their return. Frank seemed to be cheap with everything and everybody, except himself. He spent heaps of money on Savile Row suits, and all of his shirts were custom-made. Of course the car was the best example of his desire to show the world how successful he was. Yet, he expected his wife to press his trousers for him. It was such a peculiar dichotomy. Anne had trouble not laughing about it. Still, she had vowed for better or worse. All marriages had little peculiarities. Why should hers be any different? The other trait in his personality that she'd begun to notice was his propensity to throw little jibes in to her about the aristocracy. It seemed that nearly every sentence began with something about how Anne had been raised by a Duke, and in his world things had been different.

Just before noon, her phone rang. It was Frank. He wanted to know if she'd like to meet him in the store tearoom for lunch. Of course, she said yes. Obviously he'd recovered from his grumpiness. They met at the entrance and requested a table for two. Several people glanced around when they entered. Everyone in the store knew they'd just been married, which made the couple a topic of conversation. Frank held the chair out for her, and she smiled sweetly at him. All seemed normal.

After they sat down and ordered, Frank began to speak.

"Anne, I apologize. I shouldn't have taken the car incident out on you. That was wrong of me. I know it could have happened anywhere. It didn't happen only because you wanted to go out to eat. I acted like a jerk."

"Well – um – yes, you did," she smiled. "But I understand and you're forgiven. Let's just put it out of our minds and get on with our lives."

"I'm with you on that. Did you have a busy morning?" he asked.

"Yes. Quite. We have lots of requests for shows. It looks like I'll be snowed under from September through Christmas."

"I'll be busy too. Starting in October we'll begin hiring for Christmas extra help. It's always a madhouse. Then, on Christmas Eve, they'll all have to be laid-off, so I'll be here until ten o'clock, just getting their paperwork in order."

"Oh no. Do you mean we'll have to stay here Christmas Eve because of your job?"

"I'm afraid so. That's one of the drawbacks of working in retail – particularly in Personnel. Why? Does it make such a difference?"

"Yes, it does to me. I thought we'd spend Christmas at my parents' house. They always have a lovely Christmas Eve dinner, followed by church, gift opening and the like. If you have to work that late, we can't possibly join them. They'll be so disappointed."

"It can't be helped. Supposing you ask them to come to London this year? I'll try to get away as early as possible, and you can do the dinner at our house, perhaps on Christmas Day. I think that might be nice."

"Yes. I do, too. I suspect they'd like that. Mummy could let the help spend Christmas with their own families. I'll take on the task of dinner. We'll put a large tree up in the drawing room, and decorate the entire house. It would be very festive."

"How do you do gift exchanges with your parents?"

"How do you mean?"

"Well, surely you don't expect to buy a lot of gifts for them. In our family, we drew names. For instance, if I got one of my sister's, I would buy her a gift. We put a money limit on them, too."

"I can see why you'd do that in a large family. It's the sensible thing. But, Frank, there'll only be the four of us. That would make for a very slim Christmas gift exchange. Everyone would receive only one gift."

"Yes. Well, really there's no need for more. I'm sure your parents don't expect anything. They wouldn't want us spending our hard-earned money on presents for them."

"The presents don't have to be elaborate, Frank. It's just the fun of having several packages to open."

"I don't agree. Anyway you work it out, if we get into buying what – three or four gifts per person – it gets expensive. At the least, I think we should set a budget and vow not to exceed it."

"I suppose that would be all right. How much did you have in mind?"

"Oh, say one pound per gift. That would be a three pound outlay per person."

"Frank. What on earth can be bought for a pound? The perfume my mother wears costs more than that."

"Yes, well, it's the thought that counts. That's what I've always been told."

"I'd be embarrassed giving my parents such inexpensive gifts, after all they've done for us. My goodness. We wouldn't even have a house to invite them to if my father hadn't bought it."

"Oh, so now I'm not a good provider. Is that it?"

"Frank, do stop being so silly. I never said anything about whether you're a good provider. You have plenty of money, that's for certain. The only thing I take issue with is your lack of desire to spend it on others."

"All right, Anne. That's enough. I think we'd better drop this topic for now. The holidays aren't even close yet. Let's see what sort of bonus I get this year."

"That's fine, Frank," Anne murmured. It seemed they couldn't discuss anything without money coming into the conversation. She didn't remember it being this way when they were seeing one another before marriage. They finished lunch in silence, and Frank announced that he had an interview waiting for him. He gave her a peck on the cheek and was off. The waitress presented the bill to Anne. The total was six pounds. She handed the girl ten pounds and left, feeling superb.

They were both so busy during the next few months, and things went along quite smoothly. In September Anne surprised Frank with a Trouser Press for his birthday, thus solving two problems. She would no longer have to figure out how to sneak the trousers out to be done correctly, and he would always have perfectly creased pants

Anne also solved the Christmas conundrum. She simply told Frank that she'd take care of all of the Christmas shopping. It would have to come out of her salary, but it was worth it to her. She bought to her heart's content. She found a lovely silk blouse for her mother, along with her favourite perfume. She also purchased a hand knitted cardigan and a beautifully coloured Hermes scarf. She found a cashmere jumper for her father and ordered two of his favourite shirts from his shirt maker. She also found a couple of good suspense novels, which were his favourite. Frank was her biggest dilemma. She wondered what, if anything, he would give her? Finally, she decided on a cashmere jumper, a pair of gold cufflinks, with his initials engraved on them, and something she knew he'd always wanted – a fancy wristwatch. She knew he wouldn't be nearly as extravagant with her, but didn't care. She truly wanted it to be a happy Christmas for her husband. Anne felt as though she'd been blessed with so much all of her life. Now it was time to enjoy giving to someone she loved.

And she did love him. With all of his odd quirks and strange personality traits, she still saw through to the real Frank. His upbringing had clearly left its scars, and she knew that she sometimes made excuses for his bad behaviour. However, their life was smoothing out, and she was glad she'd married him. More and more she began to think about having a child. She disliked the idea of bringing the subject up because she knew, beyond a shadow of a doubt, that he'd vehemently refuse to even think about it. In her heart of hearts, she didn't think he'd ever be ready to start a family. She worried about what would happen if she simply turned up pregnant. The birth control contraptions didn't always work. The thought made her nervous. What could he do if that happened? He loved her. She was sure of that. After he held a tiny little miracle conceived in love, wouldn't he be a potty over a baby as she'd be.

Anne detested the diaphragm he'd made her get, but strictly complied with Frank's wishes. She had no intention of cheating with its use, even though the idea of a baby was growing stronger. But then, something happened that removed the decision from her shoulders. One night, before Christmas, when the tree was standing tall, and all of the lights twinkled, they cuddled on the sofa. One thing led to another. She totally forgot to prepare for the lovemaking session, and didn't mention it either. Anne had no idea what the result would be. She had not consulted the calendar, and didn't have the slightest idea about whether it was a good or bad time for conception of a child.

Christmas was wonderful. Like a small boy, Frank spent days crawling around under the tree, looking at the wrapped gifts. When he saw more than one for him, he tried to entice her to give him a clue, but she refused. He shook packages, and smelled them, to no avail. On Christmas Eve when he came home from work, he had some articles for her. He'd had them all professionally gift wrapped at the store, which impressed Anne because she knew it cost extra money to do so. She planned a lovely Christmas feast of turkey, stuffing, mashed potatoes, gravy, peas, and Christmas pudding, but because Frank had to work, she served oyster stew that evening. They would attend church in the morning, and then return for their Christmas meal. So, on Christmas Eve, they ate their stew and retired to the drawing room to open gifts. Everyone was delighted with what they received. Frank went bonkers over the watch and didn't scold her for spending such a large amount of money. Perhaps he was learning. Finally, Anne opened her gifts from him. He'd given her a pretty, lacey nightgown with a matching robe, a sweet silk blouse with ribbons and ruffles, and a gold key on a chain, with the top part fashioned to look like a heart. That part was set with garnets, her birthstone. It was a sweet piece of jewelry, and she was touched. He helped her put it on, and she wore it for the rest of the holiday.

After the New Year came and went, Anne began to wonder if she were pregnant. If so, it was probably only about four or five weeks. She had no intention of telling anyone until she had verification from a physician. She was thrilled at the prospect and knew her parents would be. Unfortunately, she was not at all certain that her husband would be.

11

Anne visited the doctor in Whitfield Cove when she drove down to see her parents for her Mother's birthday on March 10, 1948. She knew by then that there was no mistake. By his calculation, she was about three months along. Frank was driving down the next day. They were planning a dinner to celebrate Lady Caroline's forty-third birthday. Anne had spoken to her mother on the phone before leaving London. She asked her to set up an appointment with old Dr. Fate, who had brought Anne into the world. Anne adored him and didn't want any other physician taking care of her.

When she arrived at Meadowlands, at about one o'clock, her mother informed her that she should stay in the car, for they were due at the doctor's surgery at half past one. Lady Caroline hopped into the car and off they went to Dr. Fate's office. They chatted a bit on the way.

"Does Frank suspect anything yet?" Lady Caroline asked.

"He's not said a word. Luckily I've been perfectly healthy. No morning sickness, no dizziness. I would think he'd be aware that there's been no monthly in quite a while, but he hasn't said. I'll be very glad to have the doctor give me his advice. I don't know what I can and can't do."

"Anne, dear. You do think Frank will be all right with this, don't you?" Lady Caroline's voice had a note of concern.

"Oh yes, Mummy. Frank's a dear man. It's sooner than we planned, I know, but he'll be fine. I'm so excited I could burst. I've waited for this all of my life."

"I know you have, dear. I want everything to go perfectly for you."

"It will, Mummy. I'm certain it will."

They reached the doctor's surgery and went in. Dr. Fate recognised her at once, although he hadn't seen her for some time. They chatted for a few moments before he put her into a room where he examined her and took samples for a pregnancy test. After he left her, and said she could get dressed. He'd return in a tick. When he came back, he was smiling.

"Well, Mrs. DeLuca, you're going to be a mother. Only about three months along, I'd say. I've calculated, and your due date should be about July 15. I did a test that will confirm it without a doubt, but I have to send the sample away. It will take a few days. Possibly a week. But, from my manual examination, there's no doubt."

"Oh, how wonderful," Anne shouted, tears streaming down her cheeks. "I'm over-the- moon. Wait until Frank finds out."

"I take it your husband isn't yet aware of this happy news?" Dr. Fate asked.

"No. I wanted to be absolutely certain. Does everything look all right to you? Nothing is amiss, is it? What restrictions am I under?"

"You're fit as a fiddle. Don't take any medication without asking me first. Of course, no horseback riding, or other strenuous activity."

"Don't worry. Nothing is going to hurt my baby. When shall I plan on seeing you again?"

"In a month. I'll see you monthly until we arrive at eight months, and then weekly. If you feel any cramping or other odd sensations, ring me at once. Congratulations to you and your husband, Anne. I know you're going to be a very happy family."

"Oh, thank you so much, Dr. Fate. I promise I'll be good as gold."

On the way home, Lady Caroline asked Anne to stop the car at a precious shop called *The Stork is Coming*. It sold maternity clothing.

"Come, let's go in. I'm going to buy out the shop," said Lady Caroline.

"Oh. What fun," Anne answered. She'd forgotten all about the fact that Frank didn't even know yet. Maybe she'd wear a maternity dress the next day when he arrived at Meadowlands. That would be a fine way to tell him. She laughed aloud.

They spent the afternoon buying six darling maternity dresses. Since the majority of her pregnancy would be in the spring and summer months, she bought pretty, warm weather fashions. She also purchased a pair of maternity pants, the newest thing on the market, with some lovely matching tops. They'd be wonderful for days at home. After nearly buying out the shop, they hurried back to Meadowlands. Anne took all of the purchases to her room, rehearsing in her head how she was going to tell her husband the news. She knew his great concern about money, but it was a totally unrealistic fear. Still, she'd need to keep that in mind when speaking to him. She didn't expect him to be thrilled, and that made her sad. It was a time in a couple's life when both should be overjoyed. But she knew the reason why he probably wouldn't be, and she vowed to try to be understanding, even if he became nasty. The thought of Frank turned her mind to that of his family. She'd *still* never met them. They'd been married over half a year, and now a baby was on the way. It didn't seem right that his parents had never met their daughter-in-law. No matter how gruesome they might be – and according to Frank they were very gruesome – it was time to meet them. If she waited too much longer, her pregnancy would be a factor in travel, so she intended to speak with Frank about that subject as soon as possible.

When he arrived the following day, he looked to be in a fine mood – handsome and perfectly turned out. His trousers were impeccably creased, and there wasn't a hair out of place. "Thank God for the trouser press," Anne giggled to herself. He gave her a nice hug, and they went in search of her parents. Both were in the library, going through an old book on the ancestry of the Whitfield family. Anne had asked her mother to get it out. She wanted to look at past names, to see if any might be suitable for the baby.

They glanced up expectantly when Anne and Frank entered the room. Anne's father came round from the desk and shook Frank's hand heartily. He'd been warned not to say anything about the baby, knowing Anne hadn't told her husband yet. Lady Caroline followed suit with a giant hug and kisses on both cheeks. Frank always looked a bit ill at ease when her parents were effusive with affection. Anne supposed it was because his parents had been lacking in that area. She wanted him to become accustomed to lots of hugs and warmth. It was important that her child grow up in that sort of environment.

⁓

It was a raw March evening, and the servants had fires roaring in every room. The foursome sat down in the library and ordered drinks. Anne didn't feel like anything alcoholic. Her stomach was a bit queasy. She asked for water with lemon.

Frank looked perplexed. "That's unusual, Anne. Are you feeling all right?"

"Yes. Right as rain. My tummy is a bit upset. Nothing to worry about," she replied.

"Right," he replied. "Actually, you've added a few pounds lately. Drinks can put on weight."

Anne was stunned at his cheeky comment. If she'd added weight, it was due to the pregnancy. Of course he didn't know that, but it was still a cheeky remark to make, especially in front of her parents.

"I think Anne looks splendid," her father intervened. "She needed a bit of weight. She's fairly glowing. You must be treating her well, Frank," he laughed.

"I do try, Lord A." Frank continued referring to her mother and father as Lord A. and Lady C. Anne had tried to get him to soften it, by at least saying Mother C. or Father A, but he wasn't having it. Anne didn't care for it, but she had bigger fish to fry.

After drinks in the drawing room, they all went to their bedrooms to change for a lovely dinner at *Chez Chloe* in Thornton-on-Sea. The restaurant was doing a booming business, and Josef Lisak was fast becoming a chef of renown. There'd even been a large article in the *London Times* about him.

While upstairs, in their suite of rooms, Anne made up her mind to tell Frank about the baby. She'd thought it over carefully and come to the conclusion that it was the best time. Her parents were there, which would keep the topic from becoming volatile. She knew her husband well enough to be fairly certain he wouldn't throw a scene in front of his in-laws.

As she sat at the dressing table, re-doing her hair, she remarked on his comment about her weight.

"Frank, your reference to my weight made me think it's time I told you something," she began.

"What, Anne? Don't tell me you're going on some silly fad diet. You haven't gained that much. It was just said in jest. I'm sorry if I offended you."

"No, I'm not going on a diet. In fact, I'm afraid I'll be gaining a good deal more weight. But it will only be temporary, darling. I found out today that we're going to have a baby."

Frank had been in the midst of tying his tie. His face turned ashen, and the tie fell to the floor. Turning toward her, he simply stared in silence. After nearly two minutes, he spoke.

"If this is a joke Anne, I don't like it. You're well aware of my feelings about having children."

Anne stood and went to him. Putting her arms around his neck, she raised on tiptoe and kissed his cheek.

"Darling, I wouldn't jest about something this important. I saw Dr. Fate today – our old family doctor. He confirmed it. I'm so happy, Frank. I know it's sooner than we'd planned, but what difference does that make? Oh please, say you're happy, too. We'll have such fun planning and preparing. You'll make a wonderful father."

Frank tore her hands away from him.

"You've done this on purpose. I should have known to expect something like this, ever since the conversation we had some months back about babies. I told you then that if you became pregnant before I was ready to have children, I'd expect that you not have it."

"Frank! How can you say such a thing? Are you alluding to an abortion? My God, Frank. Think what you're saying. You'd kill your own flesh and blood? And why? Because you don't think you're ready to be a father? Because you want to get a yacht, or go on a Grand Tour? How selfish of you. It is unfair to say I did this on purpose. I know exactly when this happened. It was that night we put up the Christmas tree. We both got carried away. You're every bit as responsible as I am. You're thirty-four years old Frank. I'm twenty-six. It is time to grow up. Now, please stop saying things that hurt me."

"Baby or no baby, I'm not giving up the things I want in life. I didn't marry you thinking I'd have to support you, let alone a baby."

Anne slumped down on the side of the bed. His words were excruciating. He'd just admitted that the only reason he'd married her was for money.

"You didn't expect to support me?" she echoed. "What do you mean by that remark, Frank?"

"It was a slip of the tongue. I shouldn't have said it. But really, Anne, your father is one of the wealthiest men in the land. What husband would expect he'd have to shell out his own money, when your father is perfectly capable of supporting both of us?"

"Are you daft? I told you before we married that I expected us to support ourselves. My parents are the most generous people in the world. They undoubtedly *would* support us if I wanted them to. But why would I do that? Have you no shame? You're a physically fit, well-educated man. There's no reason in the world why you shouldn't support your own wife. My God, Frank. My father bought us a house that we could never, ever have afforded. What more do you expect? And anyway, what in the world does this have to do with the child I'm carrying?"

"Children cost money, providing food, clothing and an education. I suppose you'll think it should have a nanny. You'll probably want to stop working to stay home and be a mother. I'm not having it."

Anne was livid. She instinctively put her hand on her tummy.

"Well, you *are* having it, whether you like it or not. All you care about is your stupid car, which cost more than I earn in a year. You act like a child I don't intend to argue this with you, Frank. I'm pregnant, and you're going to be a father. That's the way it is. Grow up."

"What gives you such a death grip on maturity, Anne? You lived at home until you were twenty-three. You should have been out on your own long before that. You're a spoiled brat. And now you want to bring another one of your ilk into the world. I should never have married. All I needed was a house. That's the only enjoyment I've had out of this marriage."

Anne was weeping. "I can't believe you're saying such hateful, evil things to me. Frank. Please stop and think. It isn't just the two of us now. There's a baby involved in this. For the sake of the child, we need to stop saying hurtful things to each other."

"I don't care for your attitude, Anne. I've told you what my feelings are. I do not want a baby. I'm not giving up my dreams for a child."

Anne collapsed her head onto the pillow, sobbing. "Oh, you god-awful, horrible person. Get out. Just get out. Leave me alone. Apparently I made the biggest mistake of my life when I married you. Leave me alone. Go back to London."

"That's fine with me," he replied.

There was a gentle knock on the door. "Anne – Frank? Is everything all right? I'm sorry to interfere, but I can hear you weeping, Anne. Frank your voice is raised. What's going on?"

"Oh, Mummy. Come in," Anne sobbed.

Lady Caroline opened the door. Anne was still weeping into the pillow, and Frank was jamming things into his travel bag, with a very angry look on his face.

"What in blazes? Is this about Anne's pregnancy, Frank?"

He whirled around toward her.

"I might have known she'd have told you about it. That's nice. I'm *only* her husband."

"Don't be ridiculous, Frank. I took her to Dr. Fate. Of course I know. What exactly is this all about?"

Anne raised her head from the pillow.

"It's about the fact that Frank doesn't want the baby. He's just told me that 'baby or no baby, he's not giving up the things he wants in life'. He also said he 'didn't marry me thinking he'd have to support *me*, let alone a baby'."

Lord Adrian Whitfield also entered the room.

"Are you barking mad, Frank? What sort of husband would say something like that? Certainly not one who loves his wife."

"I agree. I didn't sign on for a cow of a wife, waddling about, big as a house with a baby. I married a pretty, slender, beautiful lady. I even noticed that she has some spots on her face."

"Frank. That's cruel. Spots are common in pregnancy. Her body is undergoing a lot of changes. What absurdity. A woman is at her height of beauty during pregnancy," Lady Caroline snapped.

"Rubbish. I watched my mother turn into an old woman overnight due to pregnancies. Don't tell me about how beautiful the condition is. It makes me ill."

"Frank. You may leave this house at once. It's obvious that a great mistake has been made here. You know you have just as much responsibility for the creation of this child as Anne did."

"I'm sure she did it on purpose. I was just a sperm donor."

Anne sat up again. This time she screamed.

"Get out! Get out! I never want to see you again. You can expect to hear from my solicitor. Of course I won't be able to divorce you while I'm pregnant, but as soon as the baby is born, I shall. Don't worry about having to support me, let alone a baby. You won't have to do either."

Frank picked up his bag and sauntered toward the door.

"Move fast, you bastard, or by God you'll not be making any other children," shouted Lord Adrian.

Frank picked up his pace. As he ran down the staircase, he began to shout.

"These people are threatening me with bodily harm."

He was out of the door in under a minute.

12

Anne was in shock. Lady Caroline and Lord Adrian were also dumbfounded. How could such a happily anticipated event have turned upside down so quickly? There was no question in any of their minds that learning of the pregnancy had been more than a surprise to Frank. It had brought out his deepest feelings, and the truth about how he felt toward his wife. Alex had been right. He'd married Anne for money. He was a climber. It must have been quite a shock for him to learn that he was expected to actually act like a married man, and support his wife. How could Anne have been such a fool? But, the much more important question remained. What was going to happen to her now?

Her mother sat next to her on the bed. She wrapped her arms around her and also wept.

"I'm so sorry darling. I could never imagine any man reacting in such a fashion to the news that he was to be a father."

"Damned fool needs to be horsewhipped," Lord Adrian shouted.

"Adrian, hush. We've had enough upset. Anne is in a bad way. I'm going to ring Dr. Fate, and have him come by the house. She needs to calm down."

"No, Mummy. Please don't. It's your birthday. We were here for a celebration. I'm so sorry you had to witness this."

"Stop that this minute Anne. I'm glad you were here at Meadowlands," answered her mother. "God only knows what he might have done if it had just been the two of you."

"Has he ever harmed you, Anne?" her father asked.

"No, never. I don't think he'd do anything like that. He's screamed, yelled and said cruel things, but never anything physical."

"Well, obviously, you're leaving him," said Lady Caroline.

"Mummy. I don't know what I'm going to do. I'm pregnant. Don't forget that. Even if Frank doesn't want the baby, I do. I can't just run off and leave him. I have to think about the baby. I feel like I must try one more time, before I decide there's absolutely no hope."

"Anne, I don't want you going back to that house. In the frame of mind he's in, anything could happen," Lord Adrian cautioned. "If you go back to London, I'm coming with you."

"No, Father, no. We can't talk with another person present. I need to give him time to sort everything out. Then I'll go back, and try to talk some sense into him. He isn't acting rationally. Perhaps I can make an appointment for us to meet and talk to the vicar. He'd be used to dealing with this sort of problem. That way there'd be a third person present."

"Anne, dear, I cannot imagine you wanting to return to any man who has said such horrible things to you. Why, he practically said that he'd married you because of money – that he thought your father and I would be supporting both of you."

"I know. But, perhaps he didn't really mean it. He was awfully upset. Anyway, I do have to try. For the baby's sake I have to be absolutely certain in my own mind that there isn't a chance we can work this out. I'm not going back immediately. Let him get sorted out. Let him see if he misses me. In the meantime, I'm going to ring his parents. I've never even met them, or spoken to them. Perhaps they can shed some light on why he's acting this way."

"He's acting this way because he's a complete horse's arse," said Lord Adrian. "You're my daughter, Anne. I'm not going to have you treated this way."

"Father, I understand your love for me. I also know that the things he said made you very angry. Of course they did. They made me furious. But if there's any chance of sorting it out, I have to try."

Finally her parents stopped arguing. She asked to be left alone, and they acquiesced.

"Call us if you need us, Anne. We'll be downstairs in the library," said Lady Caroline. "Can we get you anything before we leave you?"

"No, I'll be fine. I just need to be alone to sort through my own thoughts."

They both gave her a cuddle and a kiss on the cheek before they left. She snuggled into her bed and wept. It was hard to imagine a worse dilemma. She'd never dreamed Frank would react like this to the news he was going to be a father. She'd heard of men who didn't always react positively when given such news, but to say the things that he had said was way over the top – in front of her parents, no less. He'd obviously lost complete control. She glanced at the clock on her bedside table. It was just after ten o'clock in the evening. It was too late to ring the vicar, but she intended to do so first thing in the morning. She also intended to ring the elder DeLucas. It was past time for her to speak to them. Whether she wanted to negotiate the trip to Newcastle was another matter, but a telephone conversation would be a start.

Anne asked herself if she still felt love for Frank, after the way he'd acted. She couldn't really answer the question. She loved the Frank she'd married, but he seemed to have changed so quickly after the wedding. Unless everything went according to his dictums, there was trouble. He obviously had a strong need for control. There were definitely big problems with money, and, in her opinion, he was exceedingly immature. It was amazing when she thought about it that Frank got on so well in his job. But, he wasn't emotionally vested in his work. He seemed to have firmly ingrained the rules necessary to get ahead in business, and he followed them to a tee. But Anne wondered about his emotional side. Had he ever loved her? Or was she nothing more than another *thing* he wanted in his climb toward success? Alex really did seem to have been right. Why, oh, why had Anne been in such a hurry to tie the knot? She should have waited. Alex had been right about Anne being on the rebound from Avery Banister. She shouldn't have been contemplating marriage to anyone. She'd been depressed and hurting. Deciding to get married had been a way to bring her out of the abyss into which she had sunk. How could she have been such a fool?

There was no way she wasn't going to have the baby. If necessary she'd have it alone. Elise Thornton had done that with Chloe. If Elise could do it, then so could Anne. She, at least, had her parents. Anne would ring the vicar, meet Frank at the church and see what could be accomplished. If there was no change in his attitude, she'd remain at Meadowlands until the baby came and then divorce him. Surely there'd be no difficulty obtaining a divorce. Her parents had heard every word he said.

Anne turned over and finally fell asleep, as the sun began to come up. Her pillow was drenched with tears.

***

She slept surprisingly well, considering her state of mind. There was no question that she was exhausted. At ten o'clock, a tray was brought to her, and while she didn't feel like eating, she forced herself for the sake of the baby. Then she pulled the telephone from the side of the bed and rang the vicar at the Anglican Church. He was very kind. She didn't go into explicit detail, but managed to give him the gist of the story. He tried to soothe her, saying it wasn't unusual for men to react in a less than stellar way when told their wife was expecting a baby. He said he'd be happy to sit down with the two of them whenever she wished. She told him she wasn't certain when it could be arranged. She'd have to work it out with Frank, but tentatively made an appointment for the next afternoon. Frank would just have to take time off from his job. If his marriage meant anything to him at all, he would be there.

After that, Anne rang the Operator and asked for the number of a Frank DeLuca in Newcastle upon Tyne. There was no Frank DeLuca listed, but there was a Francis. She knew Frank was named for his father, so it had to be the correct DeLuca. Francis was his true given name. She knew that the family had a telephone, since Frank had once mentioned paying for it. She put through the call, somewhat nervously. She had no idea what to expect from these people. A woman's voice answered the telephone. She sounded pleasant enough, so Anne went forward.

"Mrs. DeLuca, my name is Anne Whitfield DeLuca. I'm your son Frank's wife. It's shameful never to have met you, and I apologize for that. I've asked Frank on many, many occasions to name a time when we could meet, but he's always been very stubborn about doing so. I feel it's time we spoke. I'm going through a bad patch and thought you might be able to help me."

"Why, Anne. How lovely to hear your voice. Yes, I'm Rose DeLuca, Frank's mother. His father and I have been rather confused by his actions. We, too, have wanted to meet you very much. But Frank told us that you're of the aristocracy and don't associate with people of a lower class."

"Mrs. DeLuca – Rose – if that were so, then why would I have married your son? He isn't nobility. I can't imagine his having said such a thing. I'm not a bit like that. It pains me to think that you've been living with that picture of me."

"You certainly don't sound like that sort, but it's what Frank told us. We do know our place, Anne."

Rose DeLuca's English was perfect. They might be a coal mining family, but they were obviously not illiterate.

"Rose, would you mind if I were to ask you a few questions? I'm perplexed about several things."

"Of course not. We have nothing to hide."

"First, I want to be honest with you. I've just learned that I'm three months pregnant with Frank's baby. I'm thrilled, as I hope all new mothers are, but Frank has gone round the bend. He adamantly states that he doesn't want the child, and has gone so far as to say that he expects me to terminate the pregnancy. Of course I'll never do that. I know Frank is the eldest of nine children, so I can see where a baby would represent something different to him than it does to me. But I'm having a very hard time understanding his behaviour. Can you shed any light on it?"

"Frank *is* the eldest of my nine children. Each of them was planned, and all are loved. We're staunch Catholics. Frank never lost out on anything because of the number of brothers and sisters he had. We're not members of the gentry, of course, but my husband owns several coal mines, and we do quite well. Each of my children has gone to a public boarding school – well, except for Frank. All have, or will have, a university education, just as Frank did."

"Why did Frank not attend boarding school?"

"He choose not to. He was a day student. He wasn't happy as a boy."

But Mrs. DeLuca, Frank told me that his father is a coal miner. He never said anything about his *owning* mines."

"Sometimes, I don't understand that young man. He's done this sort of thing before. He likes to make people think he comes from less than he does. I suppose it makes him look like he's accomplished great things on his own. Yes, technically, his father *is* a coal miner, but there's a difference between owning the mine, and only working in it.""

"Well, of course there is. Oh my goodness. I'm stunned. I wonder what else he's been untruthful about. He told me he supported himself through university. He says he saw very little of you from the time he started school. When I wanted to meet you, to invite you to our wedding, he said he scarcely has any contact with you and that it would be very odd if he suddenly popped up and invited you to his wedding."

"Rubbish. He may be my son, but he has a problem with the truth. Frank lived at home the entire time he was at university. Even after he went to London, he still brought his laundry home every couple of weeks. He's always said I'm the only person who can press his trousers correctly. Finally his father put a stop to that. He felt that Frank was making a decent enough salary to afford to have his pants sent out to be pressed, and he wasn't having me do it anymore."

Anne felt light-headed. What in the world was going on? Had she been lied to from the very beginning? She didn't understand why he would have done such a thing. Anne asked his mother if she could explain her son's behaviour.

"Frank has always cared about appearances. He wanted us to send him to Oxford or Cambridge, but that was out of the question. We're a comfortable, middle-class family, but with nine children we'd be hard-pressed to give them that sort of education. Isn't your father a Duke, Anne?"

"Yes. He's the Duke of Kenbridge. My family lives in a small village — Whitfield Cove."

"Frank has always bragged that his goal was to gain entry to the aristocracy," his mother replied. "I'm sorry to be so blunt. As far as his attitude towards children, I'm not terribly surprised. He never has been fond of little ones. Perhaps it does have something to do with having been the first in a family of nine children. That's possible. But all of our other children love one another dearly – there's no resentment at all among them. They were quite hurt when Frank decided to marry without any of his family present. All of them feel that he's ashamed of them There's absolutely no reason he should be ashamed of anyone in this family. His closest brother, Anthony, is a barrister. Paul is a Priest. Our eldest daughter is a teacher. To be honest, Frank's father and I were hurt, and offended, when we weren't asked to your wedding."

"That isn't the way I wanted it, Mrs. DeLuca."

"Please, call me Rose. After all, you are my daughter-in-law. I've seen your photo. You're very lovely."

"That's more than I can say. I've never even seen a photo of your family."

"I'm dreadfully sorry for you. It seems Frank has been less than forthcoming."

"Yes it does, Rose. He *did* serve in the Army during the war, didn't he?" Anne was beginning to wonder whether anything he had told her was true.

"No, Anne, he didn't."

"But – but – he told me that he was at most of the great battles – D-day, The Battle of the Bulge, and so forth. He said he was an officer in the British Expeditionary Forces."

"Anne, Frank was judged unfit for the service. You see, he weighed over twenty-one stones at the time. His obesity kept him out."

"Frank weighed over twenty-one stones? That's impossible. He's very trim."

"Yes, he is now. He went on a starvation diet and lost an enormous amount of weight. He dieted all through the war. That's also when he was in school. Of course, he wasn't terribly popular, for a number of reasons. His weight, not serving in the war. When he got his weight down, the war had ended. He graduated from university, and was hired at Havilland's."

"But he told me he'd worked at Havilland's before the war, and then returned to them when peace came."

"No, that's not correct. He worked part-time at a small shop in Newcastle during school, and during the war years, while attending university. It wasn't an executive position. Actually, Frank's father knows someone on the Board of Directors of Havilland's. That's how he got his job. It would have been very hard to find employment, because he hadn't served in the military. After he'd lost the weight, they *did* view him as a loyal, good employee, and that's when he was hired for their executive training program. He did very well, and was promoted quickly. Of course, there weren't a lot of men to choose from. Most were still in the Military, or just being mustered out. We had three sons who fought. We lost one of them."

"I'm so sorry, Rose. This is simply unbelievable. Why do you think he felt the need to lie to me?"

"Because he was trying to impress you. Men who didn't fight were looked down upon. He also doesn't want people to know about his weight problem."

It struck Anne suddenly that she'd never seen a photo of Frank taken before the past two years or so. She remembered the boxes that had been on the floor of their room, which she had never opened on the day she was unpacking. She suspected there were photos in them, or perhaps even old clothing.

"Rose, I'm stunned. You've described a person I don't know. From start to finish, he's lied to me. Are you certain that everything you're telling me is true? I don't mean to imply that you're not being honest, but it's all so hard to take in."

"I understand. I'm sorry to be the one to tell you these things. I'm beginning to understand why he's kept you from us. Obviously he's been afraid that we'd say something without knowing the lies he's told you. Just bringing you to our home would have opened your eyes to the fact that he wasn't telling the truth. We have a very nice home, in a lovely neighbourhood. Each of our children has his or her own bedroom. Of course, most are out on their own now. We're proud of all of them. Frank is my son, and I love him. But I can't condone what he's done. His behaviour toward you is abhorrent. I'm ashamed that he'd do something like this But I can tell you, it won't make a whit of difference what I think."

"I see," replied Anne. "Well, you've been wonderful Rose. I appreciate your being so candid with me. I'm very confused. I'm hoping we're going to have a meeting with the vicar this afternoon. I'm so glad I have this information. I'm sorry we've never met. I should have insisted. But, from what you've told me, I don't think it would have done much good. There were too many lies. He'd have worried about being found out. I do hope we'll have the chance to meet someday."

"I hope so too. You sound like a very nice person. Perhaps you and Frank can sort it out, now that you know everything. What are you going to do, if you don't go back to him?"

"I'll stay with my parents until the baby is born. Then I'll divorce him. Actually, I suppose it could be an annulment, since the marriage was based on lies. Not that it makes much difference to me. I know it would to you, since you're Catholic. I'll keep in touch, Rose. I promise you'll get to know your grandchild. Whatever Frank has done, it isn't your fault. Thank you for talking to me."

"I'm glad you rang. I'll say a prayer for you. Do keep in touch."

When Anne hung up the telephone she was close to collapse. It was readily apparent that she'd never even known the man she'd married.

13

They met at the vicar's office. After her conversation with Rose DeLuca, Anne wasn't at all certain she even wanted to see Frank. But there was the baby to consider. Perhaps if he admitted to all of the lies, it could be worked out. She had grave doubts, but was willing to try.

She entered the Vicarage and waited in the sitting room adjacent to the office. While she was scanning the pages of a periodical, Frank walked in. He wore the stubborn, pouty look he got when he was unhappy. She nodded her head to him in acknowledgement and went back to her magazine. He nodded in return. No one spoke. Anne was dressed in an attractive yellow and white maternity coat dress, with a row of double buttons and long sleeves. Her hair tumbled about her shoulders in soft waves, and she looked very beautiful. Frank was dressed in a suit and tie, but didn't look wonderful. He appeared to be in need of sleep, and his usual impeccable grooming was absent. He was rumpled and his hair wasn't in place.

Soon after his arrival, the vicar's secretary invited them into the church office. Both took a seat and waited until the vicar entered. When he did, both stood up. He motioned for them to sit back down and made himself comfortable behind the desk.

"Now then, Mr. and Mrs. DeLuca. As I understand it, we're here to work out some difficulties you've encountered in your marriage."

Vicar Howe was a good-looking man in his late fifties. He'd married them. He contributed to a relaxed atmosphere by not wearing a coat and appearing casual in his black shirt and clerical collar.

"Mrs. DeLuca, why don't you go first, and try to explain what the problem is?"

"There are a number of problems, Father. More than I realised when I rang you. But the major one at the moment is that I'm three month's pregnant with our first child, and my husband doesn't want the baby."

He turned toward Frank. "Is this true? Why don't you want a child?"

"Because I don't believe we've been married long enough, and there are still things I want to do in life before I settle down to raising children."

"What sorts of things?"

"I'm very goal-oriented, Father. I believe in doing things in the proper order. I believe a person should do all of the things he or she has dreamed of before bringing a child into the world."

"And what are these things you need to do?"

"Sir, when I was young, still at university, I made a list of goals I wanted to accomplish in life. First, I wanted to graduate university. Then, I wanted to find a good job. I've done those things. Ideally, I wanted to tour the Continent, purchase a yacht, and have a country house."

"Those are quite lofty goals, son. If everybody waited to achieve those dreams, there'd be few children in the world."

"I'm not everyone. I've worked very hard to get where I am. I want to stay on my path until I've achieved everything else."

"Why did you marry, if these things were more important to you?"

"I suppose like all men, I fell in love."

"You suppose?"

"Well, to be completely honest, I'm not so certain anymore. The idea of a baby has knocked me for six. I didn't bargain on this. I feel like I want to run away."

"Have you no consideration for your wife, who is sitting right here, carrying your child? What you've just said is very cruel."

"I'm sorry. I don't mean to be cruel, but I'm trying to be honest."

"Mrs. DeLuca, how does what your husband just said make you feel?"

"If the situation weren't so tragic, I'd laugh. When he says he's trying to be honest, I have to assume it's the first time he's done so since we met."

"What do you mean by that?" Vicar Howe asked.

"I spoke with his mother, for the first time in my life, this morning. He's kept us apart, and now I understand why. Almost nothing he's told me since we met has been true. For instance, he told me that he served with the BEF during the war. He did not. He was too obese, and the Armed Forces wouldn't take him. He told me that he was virtually estranged from his family, raised in extreme poverty, the eldest of nine children, with a father who is a coal miner in Newcastle. The number of children and the town are correct. Everything else is a lie. His father isn't a coal miner. He owns coal mines. He told me he left home when he started Newcastle University. That's a lie. He lived at home all through his education. He was still taking his clothing home to be laundered after he found a very good job. I don't actually know my husband, Father Howe."

Frank's face turned bright red as the vicar asked, "How do you explain these discrepancies Mr. DeLuca?"

Frank was silent for some minutes. "I may not have been honest about everything, but they're minor things. My family are decent enough people, but they're not in the same league as my wife's family. I didn't want to be embarrassed. The same thing was true about my military experience, or rather lack of it. I didn't want to tell Anne about my weight problem. Those things are in the past. She would have wondered why I hadn't served in the war."

Vicar Howe looked down at his desk. He was clearly mulling everything over.

"I think the lies you've told are very problematic. That isn't the way you enter marriage. But they're an entirely separate issue from your attitude toward the baby your wife is carrying. That needs to be addressed first. One of the major reasons for marriage is procreation. I assume you are aware of that."

"Yes, and I planned to have children someday. Just not yet."

"Ah yes, after the European Grand Tour, the purchase of a yacht and obtaining a magnificent country home. Mr. DeLuca, it's time to put away the things of childhood – to become an adult. You're being exceedingly childish and selfish, too."

"I'm sorry you view it that way, Vicar. I don't see anything wrong with having goals in life."

"There isn't anything wrong with goals, if they're realistic. In addition, I'm greatly troubled by your obvious lack of feeling toward your wife. I have to wonder if you've ever really loved her, since your feelings seem to have changed so rapidly."

"I know, Sir. I'm wondering the same thing."

Anne had heard enough. "Frank, do you or do you not want to continue this marriage? I'm not going to sit here and be demeaned. I'm only here because there's a child involved. I swore I'd try very hard to make certain he or she has a stable, two-parent upbringing."

Frank turned to Anne. "Anne, can't we go home and try to sit down and sort this out? It's a terrible muddle. I think if we could just start at the beginning, and discuss all of our feelings, we could reach some sort of understanding. I know I've made mistakes. I'd like a chance to explain everything."

Anne thought for a moment. She wasn't at all certain she even wanted to work it out. If there'd been no baby, she knew she wouldn't. But there *was* a baby.

"All right, Frank. I'll agree to meet you at the house in London. But I'm not staying overnight. After our conversation, I'm coming back to Meadowlands. Do you think I'm making a mistake, Vicar Howe?"

"I think you have to do what you feel is right. Honestly, right now I don't hold out much hope for this marriage. But, because there's a baby to consider, you're right in making every attempt to see if there can be some solution."

"All right," answered Frank. "I'm going to leave now. I'll see you in a couple of hours in London." He shook the vicar's hand and left.

"Do you feel comfortable meeting with him alone?" he asked.

"Yes. He's never hurt me physically. I don't see that I have much choice. I need to get this resolved. Now that I've learned about all the lies he's told me, I'm even more skeptical that my marriage can go forward. But, as you say, there's the baby."

"Yes. There's the baby. Go then, but I offer one piece of advice. It's my own opinion that he's a very troubled young man. Don't say or do anything to set him off. I feel a bit uncomfortable about you going to see him alone."

"I understand," Anne answered, with tears in her eyes. "I'll be careful. I just want to resolve this one way or the other."

"Make certain your parents know where you're going."

"Yes, I shall. Thank you, Father. I appreciate you saying the things you did to him. He needs to understand that I'm not the only one who thinks he's very immature."

Vicar Howe took Anne's right hand in both of his.

"God bless you. Ring me after you've spoken with him. I'll pray that your conversation goes well."

Once Anne arrived in London, they sat in the drawing room and drank a cup of tea. The conversation started out well enough.

"Anne, I'm sorry if I've hurt you. That was never my intention. But I can't help what I feel. I'm trying to see your side of this, too."

"Well, that's a beginning, Frank, I really don't know what you expect of me. I've told you, unequivocally, that I am not going to do anything to end this pregnancy. I think it's time you faced reality. We are going to have a baby. It's due in July. I intend to work until I'm six months, and then my career is over. I want to stay home, and be a mother. We can well afford for me to do that. My father has told me the exact amount of money you received from my dowry. It was enough to make us wealthy for the rest of our lives. Once the baby comes, I expect to live like other women from our social class. I'll want a nanny, and when it's time, a governess. This baby will have everything a child should have in life. Am I making myself clear?"

Frank's face turned red again. "Who do you think you're giving orders to?" he asked.

"I'm not sure, Frank. After talking to your mother today, I'm not sure I know you at all."

"You had no business ringing my mother."

"It's the only way I was ever going to learn the truth about you. Now, on top of your peculiar attitude towards being a father, I've learned that you've been a first rate liar from the beginning."

"I've lied about nothing of any consequence."

"Perhaps you don't think so, but I do. I was completely shocked when your mother told me the truth. It takes an awfully cold person to treat his own parents in this way, only because you were terrified they'd tell me the truth about you. The ridiculous thing is that I wouldn't have cared a whit. I'm sorry you had to go through embarrassment and hurtfulness because of your weight. I'm proud of you for having done something about it. It can't have been easy. I understand more about you now that I know about it. Of course that's why you're so overly concerned about your appearance. I imagine you've always been obsessed with that."

"Don't bring up my weight. That's in the past, and it's going to stay there. I'm not that person anymore."

"Frank, are you afraid that if we have a child, it will inherit your propensity for a weight problem? Does that fit into this?"

"No child of mine will ever have a weight problem. I'd make certain it was put on a diet from the moment it was born."

"Frank, I can see why you'd be worried. I'd work with a pediatrician to make certain there was no metabolic difficulty, and of course it would follow a healthy diet. Your words concern me a bit. You sound as though you wouldn't hesitate to starve a child."

"I wouldn't. There's nothing worse in the world than being an overweight child."

"I'm sorry you had to endure that, but again, you should feel proud of yourself for beating the problem."

"Let's get off the subject of weight. I want to know how you think we're going to be able to accomplish the goals I've set, along with having a baby."

"We're going to wait, like most people do, until we can afford to do all of those things. I think your idea of a yacht is pure foolishness. Where are you going to moor it?"

"There are countless places right near your parents' house. Hopefully we'll have our own home, in the same vicinity, someday."

Frank, do you even know anything about boating?"

"No. But I can learn. I've dreamed about yachting all of my life."

Anne shook her head. "Frank, this is idiocy. I cannot imagine that you'd put more emphasis upon a yacht, than you would a baby."

"One should come before the other."

"Yes, the baby should take priority."

"Not to my way of thinking."

"We're not getting anywhere, Frank. You've said so many things that trouble me. I want an explanation for your continued statements about not being certain you even love me, not to mention the one about not thinking you'd have to support me, let alone a baby."

"I'm not one hundred percent certain I do love you. You aren't the same lady I married. I wanted a wife, not a mother."

"My God, Frank. I can be both. What a stupid thing to say."

"The thought of seeing you as big as a cow makes me sick."

"So you've already said. I think I've had enough of this conversation. This isn't going to work, Frank. I'd like you to leave."

"You want *me* to leave? This is just as much my house as it is yours. I'm not going anywhere."

"Frank, can't you at least act like a gentleman? I'm pregnant. I'm upset. Can't you just leave me alone? I don't feel like driving back to Meadowlands tonight."

"Then, go to your room, Anne. Go to your room, like a good girl."

"Are you daft? I'm not staying here with you. It's much easier for you to leave. Go to a hotel for the night."

"Oh yes. Go spend a fortune on a hotel room, when I have a perfectly fine bed at home."

"Frank, I feel sick. I'm not driving to my parents tonight. Please have enough consideration for me to do as I ask."

"I repeat, Anne. Go to your room. I don't like your attitude. You're not performing your job adequately. I don't want any more nonsense out of you."

"Frank. You really are daft." Anne stood and stared at him for a moment. His eyes had turned black, and she was a bit frightened. She wanted desperately for him to leave. She wished she'd never agreed to meet him. Her thoughts were in a jumble. The best thing was not to let him get the upper hand. 'Stay in control,' she thought to herself.

"Frank, I'm asking for the last time, will you please leave this instant?"

"No, I won't, Anne. And until you go to your room, I'm going to start breaking all of the precious things you seem to love so much. All of the items we received as wedding gifts."

He picked up a crystal ashtray and threw it across the room. It hit the fireplace and shattered. Next he picked up a Waterford crystal lamp and sent it in the same direction.

"Frank. Stop it this instant," she screamed. Anne ran over to him, trying to grab the vase he was holding. "Give that to me. Stop destroying these lovely things." She reached up and hit his arm, to make him stop the tantrum. He dropped the vase and doubled up his fist. Before Anne could step back, he'd hit her full force in the stomach. She bent over in pain.

"Stop it. Stop it," she screamed.

Anne was sobbing. But he didn't stop. The next blow sent her to the floor. He continued to pummel her, aiming directly for her stomach. She felt excruciating pain.

"Please stop. You're going to kill the baby," she gasped.

"I hope I do, you bitch," he hollered, as he swung again.

By then Anne was curled on the floor like a fetus, trying to protect her baby, but the blows kept coming. When she passed out, he picked up the keys to his beloved automobile and left.

14

When she regained consciousness, Anne knew she was in trouble. She was alone in the drawing room, bleeding. She crawled on her hands and knees to the telephone and pulled herself up on a chair, so that she could reach the receiver. She placed a call to her parents. When she heard her father's voice, she could scarcely speak through hysterical sobs.

"Daddy. Daddy. It's me, Anne. I need you. Please come and get me."

"Anne, darling. Where are you? Are you at the London house?"

"Yes, please come quickly. Frank has beaten me. I'm losing the baby."

"Anne. Call the Operator. Have them send the ambulance lads. Your mother and I will leave immediately, but it's far too long a drive. You need to get to hospital at once. Tell them to take you to St. Bart's. We'll meet you there in Trauma."

The line went dead. Anne dialed the O for Operator. When a voice came on the line, she repeated what her father had said.

"Please send help at once to St. Mary Abbott's Court. My husband has beaten me. I'm pregnant. I think I'm losing the baby."

She dropped the phone and fainted. The next time she came round, the ambulance lads were there. Frank had left the door unlocked when he'd exited, so they'd had no trouble gaining entry. Anne was hazily aware of what they were doing, as they hooked her up to oxygen and started an intravenous. Line. They put her on a gurney and carried her out to the vehicle. They sped through the night to St. Bartholomew's Hospital, with the siren wailing. Anne had never felt more alone in her life.

Throughout the long night, she alternated between shock, heartbreak, anger and despair. Thank God her parents arrived before terribly long. Lord Adrian managed to keep himself under control, but only just. It was evident that he'd have liked to thrash Frank within an inch of his life. Anne underwent surgery because there was no hope of saving the baby. The doctor assured her that she hadn't been damaged in any permanent way, which meant that she was still capable of having children. It scarcely mattered to her, since she couldn't imagine ever marrying again, or caring about someone enough to want his baby.

When she came back to her room from Recovery, Lady Caroline and Lord Adrian were waiting for her.

"Oh, my darling Anne. How can this have happened to you?" exclaimed her mother. "We should never have agreed to let you go back to that monster. What happened to set him off in such a mad way?"

"He's insane, Mummy. We met with Vicar Howe. Frank begged me to come back to London and talk to him alone. I didn't think it would work, but it seemed the only thing left to try. Vicar Howe was obviously disgusted with him. He didn't even try not to show it. By then, I'd pretty much decided we'd be divorcing. But for the baby's sake, I felt I had to give it one last try. I met him at St. Mary Abbott's Court. At first the conversation was somewhat rational, but then he became angry. Finally, I'd had enough. I told him the marriage wasn't going to work and asked him to leave. He refused. I didn't feel well and couldn't imagine driving back to Meadowlands at night. I asked him again to leave – to simply act like a gentleman. He kept telling me to go to my room, as if I were a child. Finally he started throwing things. He started breaking all of the precious crystal we had in the house. I ran across the room to try to stop him. When I grabbed his arm, he made a fist and hit me in the stomach. Once he'd done that, it was as if he'd unleashed all of his fury. He just continued hitting me over and over until I was on the floor. Then, he picked up his car keys and left. I fainted. When I came to, that's when I rang you."

"Where is the rotter now?" Lord Adrian asked, through gritted teeth.

"I've no idea. He's too cheap to pay for a hotel, and I doubt he'd return to the house. I just don't know. It would surprise me if he went to his parents in Newcastle."

"Do you want us to ring the police? He should be thrown into jail for assault."

"Oh, I don't think so," Anne cried. "If the authorities are brought in, he'll go even more bonkers. You know his job is the only thing that matters to him. If this is reported, he'll surely be let go. I know Randall Gorman, the President at Havilland's. He would never stand for this sort of behaviour. God only knows what Frank will do if he loses his job. Of course he'd blame me. I just want him out of my life."

"Anne, dear, he really should be prosecuted for this terrible thing he's done," her mother said.

"Yes, I know, but I'm frightened. I know him well enough to be certain he wouldn't take losing his job lying down. I think he'd come after me with a vengeance. I don't think he sees what he's done as having been anything that awful."

"I really do believe he's mad. What shall we do, Adrian?" Anne's mother asked, turning to her husband.

"Anne is undoubtedly correct. I hate to let him get away with this, but I don't want to take the chance of her being hurt again. You know how the authorities would treat something like this. He'd likely receive a slap on the wrist, or some short jail time. He'd be out again, and angrier than ever. It isn't as though they'd put him away for twenty years. Someday, this sort of crime should be called what it is – murder. He killed that baby as sure as if he'd taken a gun to its head."

"Yes, of course you're right. So let's get Anne well, and take her back to Meadowlands."

"What about all of my things at St. Mary Abbott's Court?" Anne asked.

"We'll take care of that, dear. You need to rest now. We're going to stay at your house tonight, just to make certain he doesn't try to come back and remove everything, or worse still, ruin the house. If you need us at any time, have the nurses ring us. Otherwise, we'll be back in the morning. We love you, Anne. None of this was your fault. You did everything you could to save the marriage and the baby. Please try to rest. The doctor said you'd be given a sedative, so that should help you sleep."

"All right," Anne answered, in a weak, defeated voice. "I just want to go home to Meadowlands. I'm sorry I ever moved to London."

By nightfall the next day, Anne was back in her childhood bedroom at Meadowlands. The doctor had been round early that morning and told her he was going to release her. He left her with a few instructions and said he wanted to see her in a week at his office. She asked if she could just see her physician in Whitfield Cove and was told that would be fine. Anne quickly placed a call to her parents, who were just getting up, telling them she'd be able to go home. They hurried to St. Bartholomew's and checked her out. By afternoon they were back in their own, safe village.

She'd heard nothing from Frank, and still had no idea where he'd gone. What's more, she didn't care. Lord and Lady Whitfield made immediate arrangements for all of Anne's furnishings to be moved from the London house, as well as her personal effects. That had already been accomplished. The only things left were furnishings from Frank's flat in Nottingham and the few wedding gifts that had come from his friends. There were none from his family, since they'd not been invited. Anne considered ringing his mother, since they'd previously spoken, but she didn't feel up to it. Anyway, she doubted he'd been in touch with them. If he returned to St. Mary Abbott's Court and saw that most everything was gone, he'd undoubtedly fly into another rage. Anne was glad she was safe at her parents' home, far from London.

She rang Alex at the office and told her briefly what had happened. Of course, Anne would not be returning to her job. Alex was furious with Frank and said she was going to quit, too.

"On no, Alex. Please don't. I expect they'll give you my job. You'd be very good at it. Don't throw away your own future because of what Frank did to me. That would only compound the damage. Please. Think about it. Don't make it easy for him. Just think how uncomfortable he'll be, knowing that you're aware of everything that happened. He'll give you a wide berth."

"I'll do whatever you want, Anne. Our friendship is more important to me than a job. I can always get another job. But if you want me to stay, I shall."

"I do want you to stay. I'd feel awful if you left. Then I'd feel like my bad decision ruined your life, too."

"Don't be daft. This isn't your fault. Place the blame where it should lie. You obviously married a madman. I'm so thankful you're safe now. Please just rest and get better. I'll be down to see you this weekend."

Anne would miss Alex. They'd become such dear friends. Perhaps the only good to come of the entire mess was that Alex would advance in her career. She wanted to think the person with whom she'd worked so closely, would continue on as the Fashion Coordinator at Havilland's. Anne hadn't had time yet to think about her own future. There were few job opportunities in her village – certainly not real career possibilities. She'd have to think about all of that.

All she knew was that she was not returning to London.

❦

Frank had driven most of the night. He alternated between total rage and tremendous sorrow. It would have been evident to anyone who spoke with him that he was in need of mental health treatment. When he was enraged, he wished he'd killed Anne. On the other hand, he wanted her back and couldn't imagine a life without her. She'd been the best thing that'd ever happened to him. They'd been just fine until the bloody baby had interfered. They hadn't needed a baby. He didn't want to share her with a baby. Why was that so important to her? Was that the only reason she'd married him – to get herself a child? That's what he truly believed. She'd used him. He should have known no one of her background would have chosen to marry someone who'd grown up in Newcastle. There had to have been an underlying motive. Naturally it never crossed his mind that Anne, being a beautiful intelligent woman, could have had her pick of any number of men – men who would have been happy to father her child. When he reached the point where he'd convinced himself that she'd targeted him as a patsy, he became filled with anger again. He vowed she wouldn't get away with what she'd done.

He thought about their house, which he loved. Would she try to take that away from him? Was she going to file for divorce? She couldn't as long as she was pregnant. Was she still pregnant? Had she called her parents? Surely they wouldn't divorce because of a silly fight. He'd make it up to her. He concentrated upon what it would be like when they made up. He needed to find a special gift for her. It was morning, and he felt fatigued after the long night of driving. He was on the outskirts of a tiny village, somewhere in Somerset. He saw a café and pulled off the road. He needed a cup of coffee and something to eat. Then perhaps he'd explore the village and see if he could find a gift for Anne.

After a decent breakfast he felt better. He'd suddenly remembered that he needed to ring the office and tell them he wouldn't be coming in. He didn't want to lie. He wasn't a liar. He'd just say that he had some personal things to attend to. It was true enough. That completed, he ambled on to the High Street and looked in shop windows. As he walked, he came upon an antique shop. In the window was a brass, baby cot. It had to be very old. He could polish it, just as he had the adult bed they'd bought. Anne would adore it. It was the perfect gift. It was tied to the boot of his car in short order, and he turned back in the direction of London. If he hurried, he'd be home by the time it was dark. Anne would be in the kitchen cooking one of her good meals. He would surprise her. Everything would be back the way it was supposed to be.

<hr />

When Frank walked into St. Mary Abbott's Court, the house was almost completely empty. He stood in the foyer and shouted at the top of his lungs. She had left him. The bitch had left him! Not only that, but she'd taken almost everything they owned. He wandered through the rooms, only occasionally coming upon something that had belonged to him before he married. She'd left the brass bed and a few other items. Was this her way of getting him out of the house? Well, it wouldn't work. The house was his. Just as much his as it was hers. It didn't matter who'd paid for it. So this was the game she intended to play. Well, Frank Deluca wouldn't be so easily disposed of. He went to the telephone and rang his solicitor. He needed sound legal advice. There was no doubt in his mind that after she simmered down, she'd come back to him. But until then, he was going to make certain nothing happened that caused him to lose his home. He'd worked all of his life to have a home like this. No one was going to take the fruits of his labour. Finally he calmed down enough to catch a few hours of sleep.

In the morning he proceeded to change into a fresh suit. All of his clothing still hung in the closet, and a pair of trousers was folded neatly on the pants press. He thought about how glad he was that he'd purchased that item. Without it, he'd have to send the trousers back out to be pressed. It had been wise thinking on his part. He bathed and shaved. When he was dressed, the doorbell rang. Frank scurried downstairs, certain Anne had come to her senses and was home. When he unlatched the lock, a found a young man standing at the entrance.

"May I help you?" Frank asked.

"Yes, Sir, if you'll sign right here. I have some papers for you."

Frank took the pen offered, signed his name, and was handed an envelope. He thanked the boy and closed the door. He proceeded to open the packet. Scanning the contents, he threw the papers on the floor. Cursing and shouting, he stomped through the downstairs. She'd served him with divorce papers. Divorce papers! Was she mad? She couldn't do this. She was going to have a baby. People couldn't divorce when the wife was pregnant. He stormed back into the entryway and picked up the strewn papers. Sitting down in a chair, he slowly read them.

She was no longer pregnant. According to these papers, he'd assaulted her and caused her to lose the child. He didn't believe it. He had not assaulted her. He might have protected himself when she hit him. That was self-defence. He'd done nothing to cause a miscarriage. He'd wanted that baby desperately. He'd even bought the antique baby cot. He got up and walked out to the car. There it was, still tied to the boot. He undid the rope and carried the cot into the house. He took it up the stairs, and put it into the spare bedroom, nearest the one he and Anne shared. That would be the baby's room. He'd need to get started polishing it. He'd do that the next weekend.

Returning to the front entry, he reread the divorce papers. He couldn't believe she was accusing him of such vile acts. She must have lost her mind. That would explain it. She'd lost the baby, and that had caused her to have a complete breakdown. Oh God, his poor Anne. He needed to go to her. He would reassure her that they could have other children. As soon as she felt better, they would try again. He needed to speak with his solicitor. If he explained the entire situation to him, he'd know how to handle this divorce nonsense. He'd help Frank find Anne. She was undoubtedly in a hospital somewhere in London. Perhaps the barrister could call her parents. Frank didn't think he should. If, by chance, she'd told this outrageous story to her mother and father, they would be angry with him. They probably wouldn't sit still long enough for him to tell them the truth.

Frank grabbed his keys and went out to the car. He was very anxious to get this matter straightened out so that Anne would come back home where she belonged.

15

John Dryden opened the door and greeted Frank DeLuca. They'd known each other since their college days at Newcastle University. Frank was a decent enough chap in John's opinion, although they'd never been close friends. Frank had suffered a terrible weight problem at university and had never socialized much. The two men were completely different sorts. John was down-to-earth, soft-spoken, sensible and rather introverted. He had an analytical mind. Frank was what John would have described as obsessed with control. John figured some of that was due to the willpower he'd needed to overcome obesity. He was much organised, but sometimes seemed scattered. John always thought Frank might suffer from mood swings, but he'd never spent a lot of time with him. He was aware of Frank's success in business and that he was climbing the ladder at Havilland's Department Store.

"Come in, Frank. I haven't seen you in ages. I heard you'd married. Congratulations. I should have sent a note when I read about it."

"No matter. That's what I'm here about. There's been a terrible misunderstanding." He handed the divorce papers to John.

John read through them. They were basically standard form. The only thing John was really interested in was the reason Frank's wife gave for taking such action. When he saw the sentence that alluded to Miscarriage and

Assault, his eyebrows shot up. This appeared to be more than a standard divorce case.

"Sit down, Frank. Would you like some tea, or coffee? I think we have both."

"No, no. I'm fine," Frank answered. "I'm just anxious to know what can be done about those papers."

"Well, first I need to know exactly what happened. Something pretty serious must have taken place in order for her solicitor to have cited these reasons for a divorce."

"It wasn't serious at all," Frank answered. "Do you want me to tell you everything?"

"Yes. Absolutely."

"All right. Anne, my wife, went down to her parents' house in Kent and visited her family doctor. He confirmed that she was three months pregnant. I was coming down later in the day. When I got there, she told me about the baby. I was over-the-top, as you can imagine."

John smiled and nodded. "Of course."

"Well, we ended up in an argument. Tell the truth, I don't even remember what it was about. I was irritated that her parents knew about the baby before she'd told me. You can understand that."

John nodded his head slightly and told Frank to go on.

"Well, the entire thing got totally out of control. You probably know how women can be when they're pregnant. I said some things I shouldn't have. Of course, I was totally stunned at the news."

"What did you say, Frank?"

"Nothing much. I told her that I wasn't going to give up the things I wanted in life just because we were going to have a baby."

"Such as . . .?"

"Such as a country house, a Grand Tour of the Continent, and a yacht. Those are all goals I'd set long ago."

"All right," John answered, looking down at the papers on his desk. "Go on."

"Well, Anne just exploded. Then her parents got into the middle of it. It became a real row. I wanted to talk to my wife alone. I didn't feel it was any business of her parents. Things were getting too heated, so I said I was leaving, and I drove back to London. The next day, we agreed to meet at the vicar's office – the one who married us."

"And did you?"

"Yes, we did. To make a long story short, that didn't go well either. I still wanted to speak with her alone. Finally, we agreed to meet back at our house in London to chat, and we did. Anne was completely undone by then. She wasn't rational. She kept trying to chat about things that had no bearing on her pregnancy. She started raving about why I'd married her – for money according to her – and saying I'd never planned to support her. Her father is a Duke, and I'm sure a lot of these ideas were planted in her mind by the parents. I was worried when we married, because of the difference in our backgrounds. I feared it might cause some difficulties. Her family is very posh. She was so upset, I couldn't talk to her sensibly, and I told her to go to her room. Just to calm down, you understand. She refused. Then she started throwing things about. Lovely things, like crystal lamps, and the like. I walked over and put my arm on hers to stop the madness. She hit my arm. I shook her, I think. Honestly, John, I don't really remember. I was so distraught. Anyway, she ended up on the floor. I thought I should just leave, and let her calm down, so I got my keys and left."

"Have you seen her since?"

"No."

"When did this happen?"

"The night before last."

"Where have you been since then?"

"I drove around all night and ended up in Somerset. Not for any reason. Sometimes, when I'm upset, it helps to drive. You know, I have a new Ferrari 125 S. It drives like a dream. Anyway, I felt terrible about the fight, but then I was also irritated that she'd started the whole thing to begin with. Finally, I decided to go home and make amends. I even found an antique, brass, baby cot in a small shop and bought it. I had to tie it on the boot of the car. I was afraid it would scratch the paint. But I was willing to take the chance, in order to surprise Anne with a gift."

"What happened when you got home?"

"She wasn't there. Not only that, but most of the furnishings were gone. She left a bed and a few other items. Not much. I can't believe she got a lorry in there so fast. All because of a stupid fight."

"So what did you do?"

"The next morning, after I was dressed, the bell rang and those were delivered," Frank said, pointing to the divorce papers. "I called your office, and now I'm here. What do I do, John?"

"Frank, there are very serious charges here. According to these papers, you assaulted her, and she miscarried as a result. That, my friend, is a prosecutable offence. I think you may need a criminal barrister. I have no way of knowing whether your wife is going to file criminal charges."

"Criminal charges? For what? I didn't do anything! I simply defended myself. If she lost the baby, it didn't have a thing to do with our silly argument. She's trying to blame me for something I didn't do."

"Are you certain, Frank? You said yourself, you don't remember."

"I'd remember if I'd beaten up my wife and caused her to lose a baby. I'm not that sort of man, John."

"I didn't think you were, Frank. Nonetheless, that's what's being alleged."

"So, what do I do?"

"Let me do some investigation. I'll contact her solicitor to find out if there are going to be any charges filed. If not, we'll proceed as though it's a routine divorce case."

"But I don't want a divorce. I want my wife back. We have a beautiful home. I don't want to lose it. What will happen to that?"

"Is your name on the deed?"

"Yes. Um, her father bought it for us as a wedding gift. It was put in both of our names."

"Whew. That's some wedding gift. Well, if it's in your name, the usual remedy is to sell the property, and divide the proceeds."

"But I don't want to sell it."

"The only thing you could do in that case would be to pay your wife half of the amount of the market value."

"Are you daft? I don't have that kind of money. The house is in Kensington. St. Mary Abbott's Court. I wouldn't be able to save that amount of money even if I lived to be one- hundred."

"Well, I hate to say it old boy, but you should have thought about that before you got into this mess."

"But it wasn't my fault I sincerely think it's hormones. You know how women can get."

"As I said, let me do some investigation. I'll have a better idea of what to advise after I've spoken to Mr. Casey – her solicitor."

"Shall I wait while you speak with him?"

"No. I'll ring you later today. You sound like you've had a rough go of it. Why don't you go on home? Give me your number and I'll speak with you later."

Frank wanted answers at once, but he acquiesced and left John's office.

John Dryden was suspicious of the story Frank had told. He had a feeling there were things left out. After placing a call to Mr. Casey, he was put through to his private line where he answered on the second ring.

"Mr. Casey. This is John Dryden. I don't think we've met before. My client, Frank DeLuca, was in to see me just now. He's quite upset about divorce papers served on him this morning. It seems they hit him out of the blue. Can you fill me in a little more about the case?"

"Certainly, John. My client, Mrs. DeLuca, was released from hospital this morning. Before she returned to Kent with her parents, she came to see me. I'm the Whitfield family solicitor. Mrs. Deluca is the former Lady Anne Whitfield. It's just as the papers state. Her husband assaulted her. She was taken by ambulance to St. Bart's. She lost the baby she was carrying. She wants a divorce."

"I suppose there are records at the hospital regarding her injuries and their cause?"

"Absolutely. I can get them for you. Or you can subpoena them. I have them here. She was pretty badly beaten up. He hit her in the abdomen several times. That entire area is black and blue with bruises. It was an obvious attempt to cause harm to the baby."

"Oh God. I was afraid of that. Is the wife going to file criminal charges?"

"I advised her to, but she's afraid of him. She says she just wants to get out of the marriage. She's frightened that if she takes this further, he'll retaliate in some way."

"She may be right. I know her husband from university. I wouldn't have thought him capable of this, but have to admit I've always thought him a bit unstable. I'm not certain I want to handle this case."

"Oh, John, don't do that. Mrs. DeLuca wants to get the ball rolling. If you don't take the case, someone else will, and he might not be as capable or sensible as you sound. I intend to treat it as a regular divorce case. She certainly has grounds. All that's necessary is a property agreement."

"Yes well, Mr. DeLuca doesn't want a divorce. He also refuses to even consider selling the home and says there's no way he could pay her half of the market value. This is bound to be prolonged and messy."

"Isn't there some way you can explain to him that he's being foolish? She'll get the divorce eventually, no matter how hard he fights. If this goes into court, he's likely to lose everything. The hospital records are damning."

"Let me see what I can do. I'll prepare his answer to the divorce, and I'll try to get it to you by tomorrow."

John Dryden hung up the telephone and put his head in his hands. He detested defending this sort of client. There was no question in his mind that Frank DeLuca had beaten the hell out of his wife and caused her to lose his own child.

16

Anne sat by the window in her room at Meadowlands. Over three months had passed since the nightmare had begun. It was spring again, and she thought back to her happiness the previous year. How could such a beautiful beginning have turned into such a nightmare? It was hard to understand why things never seemed to work out for her. Was her judgment so poor? Did she act too impulsively? Should she have listened to Alex? If she was honest with herself, she had to admit that she'd never really loved Frank. Not as she should have. Not enough to have married him. It had been too soon after the breakup with Avery Banister. Even then, Frank wasn't the right man. She'd been depressed. She wanted a home, a husband, and a child. She realised now that she'd decided to settle for less than she wanted or deserved. But still, she had learned to love him. Hadn't she? There were certainly times she'd believed she honestly did love him. She would never have wanted a baby with him if she'd thought it would end as it had.

Where did she go from here? She was nearly thirty years old. She'd been engaged once, nearly engaged another time, and married. The chances of anyone wanting her with that sort of history were slim. So what would the future hold for her? She didn't want to spend the rest of her life living like a spinster at her parents' home. Someday she'd lose them, and then what?

Some distant cousin would take over Meadowlands. Where did that leave her? She had been back in her parents' home since March, and it was time to make some decisions. She'd been so terribly depressed in the beginning. Just getting through a day had been a monumental task. But she'd managed to pull herself out of a deep abyss, and was beginning to feel stirrings of a desire to think about the future.

The divorce was going nowhere. Frank refused to budge. He didn't want a break up and stubbornly fought her on all fronts. Of course, reaching an agreement about the house was out of the question. Anne's father even counseled her to let it go – allow Frank to have it all, but Anne wasn't agreeing to that. It was bad enough that he'd been given a large amount of money from her dowry and that he would receive half of the value of the house. She adamantly refused to consider letting him have it all.

She often thought she'd made a mistake in not prosecuting him. That was the reason men got away with the sort of thing he'd done – women being frightened to take their husbands to court, not wanting to testify, or to relive the nightmare over again. Being frightened of retaliation and having an aversion to all of the publicity that would surround such a case. They were all valid reasons, but they were also the reasons why men like Frank escaped the penalty for detestable behaviour. However, it was too late now, and all Anne wanted was to move on with her life. Frank obstinately refused to allow that. He fought every attempt her solicitor made to reach an agreement of any kind. She'd never thought he could be so totally pigheaded. There wasn't much she could do but trust legal advice, and move forward in other areas. She certainly had no thought of ever remarrying, so it didn't matter much whether she was free or not. Still, Anne certainly wanted him out of her life.

When she thought about the future, there was no question that she wanted to work. But she didn't want to return to London. That meant coming up with a career possibility in the twin villages of Whitfield Cove and Thornton-on-Sea. Anne had absolutely adored her job at Havilland's, and when she finally got around to thinking about a future, she began to consider whether the likelihood existed for doing something similar in a business of her own. There was no large department store in either town, but there were many small shops, some of which carried very nice, upscale goods. Both villages were prosperous and growing after the war. With the advent of better automobiles and roads, people from as far away as London were beginning to commute to places that once were thought of as only rural communities. The villages were only a little over an hour from London, and the train service was excellent. Small towns like Anne's were becoming known as bedroom communities. People lived there and commuted to London and other larger metropolitan areas. Because of that, the idea of forming a fashion business that served as a means of entertainment, as well as fundraising, didn't seem out of the question. The idea she was turning over in her mind involved owning a firm that women's and civic groups, charities, and even large businesses might contract with to raise money for worthy causes. It didn't seem out of the question. It would take a lot of planning, but that was one of Anne's strongest traits.

She sat down with paper and pen, sketching out ideas. She'd first need a setting in which to stage fashion shows. Immediately, Josef Lisak's restaurant, *Chez Chloe* came to mind. It was a lovely spot, filled with ambiance. It was already the number one choice for dining out in the region. The first task would be to convince Josef that the idea would benefit his establishment. Of course, it would. She thought she'd begin with luncheon groups, and possibly expand to something in the order of wine dinners. She envisioned starting with perhaps one show a month, and hopefully building to more frequency, perhaps even weekly. If it was to be successful, she'd need to bring in business from surrounding villages. Perhaps even London. The trick to that would be good publicity. Since she'd earned a fine reputation while at Havilland's, Anne believed the media would give her own business good coverage. She was still in contact with the reporter to whom she'd given her first interview.

Anne would pull her fashions from shops in the area. That wouldn't be any problem, since all would like their goods showcased. She knew, from experience, that sales always increased after an item was featured on the runway. She could employ the same concept she'd used at Havilland's, using members of the charity or sponsoring the event as models. The entire concept was coming together very nicely. For the first time since the horror of losing her child and suffering through the ordeal with Frank, Anne felt optimistic. She definitely believed her concept could work. The idea of being busy again, and owning her own business, was very exciting. She even wondered if there might be a possibility that Alex would consider going into a partnership with her. It was a long shot, she knew. Alex had replaced Anne as Fashion Coordinator at Havilland's and seemed happy. Still, it never hurt to ask.

The next question was where to live? She knew she could stay at her parents' indefinitely, but that wasn't what she wanted. She'd loved living on her own and would like to do so again. Surely she could find someplace in one of the two villages that would serve her purposes. Money wouldn't be an issue. Lord Adrian would help in any way possible. Anne didn't want him to back her without something in return. He'd been generous enough with her. She would definitely let him advance the money – enough to start the business and to lease living space, but she would repay him, just as though the funds had come from a bank. She would insist that the prevailing interest rate be attached to the loan. No doubt he'd argue, but that was the way she wanted it to be.

But, first things first. Anne left her seat at the window and descended to the second floor, where she expected to find her father in his office. Before she could take any steps in the perceived direction, she'd need her father's approval. After that, she would need to speak with Josef Lisak. Anne was actually excited. She felt as if, once again, she had purpose in her life.

⚬⚬⚬

Her father loved the idea, and so did Josef Lisak. She met with him the day after she'd garnered Lord Adrian's approval. They had breakfast in a small café located on the High Street. It was the only convenient time for him, since his restaurant served both lunch and dinner. She'd always been fond of Josef, from the first time she'd met him, soon after his arrival in Thornton-on-Sea. She thought of him as a Renaissance man. He was an extremely creative chef. In addition, he spoke fluent French, English and Italian. The man was well read and intellectual, but also down-to-earth. He was easy to know. To top it all off, while he obviously had an artistic nature, Josef was very masculine. His dark hair and eyes had set more than one English girl's heart aflutter. Anne was actually surprised he'd never married. He wasn't an old man – probably in his mid-thirties. She supposed he hadn't made time for romance due to the war and his subsequent success with *Chez Chloe*. Anne had never thought of him as a potential love interest. He was Elise Thornton's brother, after all. Anne hardly thought she'd be warmly accepted into that family circle, even though she and Elise were once again friends. She knew that Josef had, at one time, loathed her, because of her interference between Sloan and Elise. At any rate, romance was the furthest thing from her mind. All of that was in the past, and Josef was a good friend. Hopefully he was also a potential business associate.

After she explained her plans to him, he immediately warmed to the idea. They were on the same page when it came to visualizing how the concept could become reality. Josef thought it was a brilliant scheme. It was one that had already proven itself at Havilland's, and he couldn't see any reason why it wouldn't work well in their small village. In fact, he felt that Thornton-on-Sea and Whitfield Cove were crying out for something of the sort. They discussed possibilities for how they could put the plan into action, exploring whether to have a set menu for people who attended the shows, or perhaps a menu that allowed three or four choices for the entrée. Anne liked the latter idea. So did Josef. It would cut down on overhead, since he would know in advance what the diners would be ordering. Rationing had finally ended, so there were no more restrictions on what food was available. He suggested selections of meat, fish and poultry in order to accommodate all tastes. They played around with the idea of offering champagne at the noon hour and wines paired with the entrée for evening shows. Anne left her meeting with him bursting with ideas and more excited than ever.

She also discussed with Josef her need for a place to live. He offered an immediate solution. Why not move into 'No Regrets'? 'No Regrets' was the quaint cottage that Elise and her daughter, Chloe, had shared with Giselle Dupris when they had first moved to Thornton-on-Sea. After Giselle had married and moved to America, Elise had lived there with Chloe and her brother, Josef. When Elise married Sloan Thornton, Joseph had stayed on. The cottage had stood unoccupied, since Joseph had moved out after Elise married Sloan. Josef loved the small cottage near the sea, but had taken up residence in quarters above the restaurant, which was perfect for his busy schedule. Sloan had purchased the cottage, since Elise loved it so much. Thus, it was no longer available for lease to outsiders. The Thorntons used it as a guest house for friends and family. Josef didn't think they would object to Anne making it her home.

Anne was a bit wary about the idea. She adored the stone cottage with the thatched roof and lovely garden, but she wondered how Elise would feel about Anne being the one to live in it. After all, she was Sloan's former fiancé, and although the rift was mended, there was still the memory of Anne's attempt to ruin Elise's happiness. Still, she and Elise seemed to have moved far beyond that muddle. Elise had even been a bridesmaid in Anne's wedding. Josef encouraged her to talk to Elise about the possibility of moving into 'No Regrets'. He felt certain she would be in favour of the idea.

So, after breakfast with Josef, Anne rang Elise, saying she needed to speak with her about a business matter. Elise, ever sweet and accommodating, agreed to a meeting. Anne told her it was about the cottage, so they chose to meet there in two hours' time. When Anne arrived, Elise was already inside the quaint, little dwelling, airing it out, and running a feather duster over the mantelpiece. When Anne entered, Elise gave her a warm smile and went to her at once. She held out her hands and took hold of Anne's.

"How nice to see you out and about. I know you've been through a frightful time. I'm so sorry. I was awfully glad to hear your voice. Am I right in assuming that you're interested in moving into this place?"

"Gosh. Aren't you perceptive?" exclaimed Anne. "Yes, that's exactly what I'm thinking. It would be perfect for me. I've always thought it charming. I know you and Giselle were happy here. I want to move out on my own. I love my parents dearly, of course, but I don't feel right about spending my life at Meadowlands. I'd like my own place."

"I don't see any reason why that wouldn't work beautifully. I'd like to know that someone is living here, and so would Sloan. Do you mind if I ask if you have any plans beyond changing addresses?"

"I do have plans. Exciting ones, I think."

Anne went on to tell Elise about the dream of opening her own company. Elise thought it was brilliant and offered to help in any way she could. Since Elise was now Countess of Wexford, following the death of Sloan's father, she was very active in community affairs. There wasn't a charitable organisaton in the village that she wasn't involved with, usually as an officer on the Board of Directors. She could be a wonderful help, sending business Anne's way.

They sat in the parlour of the cottage and chatted for nearly two hours. Anne brought her up-to-date on everything that had happened with Frank, including the current status of her divorce petition. Elise was very dear. She sincerely felt anguish for Anne. Of course, Elise had experienced heartache of her own at the hands of abusive men. Anne knew all about the gruesome attack she'd endured at the hands of three Nazi soldiers during the war. She was the perfect person to talk to about the feelings a woman experiences after that sort of violence. Elise made it clear that she wished only the best for Anne and would do anything in her power to help her recover from such a traumatic event. By the time they said their goodbyes, both ladies felt easy with one another again. They'd reached an agreement regarding the cottage, and Anne's mood soared. At first Elise had said there was no need for her to pay rent, but Anne was adamant that she wouldn't consider moving without a lease agreement. Elise finally gave in and said that Sloan would have the proper document drawn up. She gave Anne the key and told her to make it her own anytime she was ready.

As they were walking down the path together, Anne noticed the 'No Regrets' sign, and she laughed aloud.

"I don't know if that the sign exactly applies to me," she said.

Elise laughed, too.

"I know. I felt the same way when Giselle and I moved in. You know, it was originally owned by an elderly couple, and it fit them to a tee. I didn't think it fit either Giselle or me, but in the end, it actually did. I hope the same thing is true for you.

"I'd have to change it to 'Nothing But Regrets', if it were ever to apply to me.'"

17

Anne's new business, *Panache*, was an overnight success. The word *Panache* was the French word meaning to dress in a stylish, distinctive way, and Anne thought it worked perfectly for the service her company offered. She'd considered simpler names, like 'Anne's Special Events', but she wanted something with more flair. Josef was actually the one who'd come up with it when he said that the fashion shows would bring a certain *panache* to their village. After all, the man *was* French. In addition, it blended with the restaurant's name, *Chez Chloe*.

Anne was off and running. Alex didn't accept her offer to enter into a partnership because she had important news of her own. She and Elliott Woodbridge, Sloan's old friend from Oxford, were getting married. They had a small ceremony planned in the village where she'd been born, in Cornwall. Anne was so happy for her, and although she wasn't able to attend, because of commitments related to *Panache,* she sent a lovely gift and beautiful flowers.

Anne's first client was the local Animal Aid Society. They decided on a fashion show and dinner as a major fundraiser for the year. It was a bit different than anything Anne had ever done before, but offered wonderful possibilities. She decided she'd visit the local shelter, select puppies and kittens and have each model carry one as they walked the runway. Of course the animals would be available for adoption, but with a twist. They'd be auctioned off at the end of the show. The models would be drawn from the society's Board of Directors and membership list. A variation would be the participation of men. They wouldn't be professional models either, and would include the chairman and the treasurer. In all, there would be twenty models.

Anne threw herself into the planning with zeal. She'd leased offices on the High Street where *Chez Chloe* was also located, so she was able to trot back and forth to the restaurant when she needed to work something out with Josef. If he had any questions, he didn't have far to travel to her new workplace. Anne met with each of the people who'd be participants in the show and was delighted with all of them. The group had the usual representation of statures, frames, figures and physiques. They also ranged from posh women and men who came from upper-middle class environments, to regular folk who loved animals and wished to devote their time to a charity they believed in wholeheartedly. Anne loved the mixture of types, as it made the show more authentic and real.

There was also a little boy and girl – children of two of the Board members – who would act as models. She used few decorations. Usually she had one large photo or poster on the runway that told the story of the charities' mission. She knew exactly the piece she'd use for this event. Before she'd married Frank, while still a young girl, Anne had three rescue animals as pets– puppies that had been found abandoned by the side of a road. Always a great lover of animals, she'd adopted the three and loved them with all of her heart. They had been small terriers named Pippen, Pamper and Prissy. A close friend of hers had once painted a treasured portrait of the pups as a Christmas gift. It was quite large and would serve as a perfect backdrop for the show. The dogs had been painted sitting on a sofa at Meadowlands, and the artist had captured their likeness's perfectly. Because it was such a dear piece of artwork, Anne asked her friend if she'd be willing to have prints made of the painting, to be offered for sale at the event. Cynthia, the artist, said she would be only too happy to do so. There was only one gigantic problem. Anne had left the painting at St. Mary Abbott's Court. In the rush of moving, it was forgotten in an out-of-the-way room on the ground floor.

Once the idea of using the painting popped into her head, Anne was not about to change her mind. It was absolutely perfect. On top of that, she wanted it back. If Frank had been a normal person, it wouldn't have been a problem. She'd have rung and told him she wanted it. But Frank was anything but normal. She knew he'd insist upon being present when she came to collect the painting. The last thing she wanted was any face-to-face meeting with him. If she tried to send someone else to get it, Anne knew he would refuse. She pondered the problem, finally deciding on a trip to London. She would go to St. Mary Abbott's Court and get the painting while Frank was at work. She still had a key to the house. The chances were high he'd never even know she'd been there. Anyway, she had a perfect right to enter the home whenever she wished, since it was still in her name, too. She wouldn't need the painting until just before the show date, so there was time to think about her plan.

Everything fell into place nicely. She and Josef spent a lot of time working together, choosing menu selections and wine, since it was to be an evening event. It was important to both of them that the show come off without a hitch, since it was the first of its kind in Thornton-on-Sea. Its success or failure would set the stage for *Panache's* reputation.

As they spent more and more time together, Anne couldn't help realizing that her feelings for Josef were growing. What she didn't know was that he felt the same way about her. Neither said a word to the other. Anne was much too wary of men. She knew Josef well, and had known him a long time, but she still had vast problems with trust. She was also terrified of rejection.

Josef, on the other hand, would never have allowed himself to think someone like Anne, a Duke's daughter, would be interested in him. He'd never suffered from a lack of self-esteem, and was comfortable with all sorts of people, but he also knew his place. Even though his sister had married into the aristocracy, and was now Lady Elise Thornton, the two had come from humble beginnings. He was drawn to the same interests, which included gourmet food, fine wine, art, and beautifully decorated homes, and he enjoyed people with similar tastes. Those people generally were found in the upper classes. No matter how educated and refined Josef was, he he'd never have presumed that Anne might find him attractive. While Elise came from the same unpretentious start, and was no more aristocratic than her brother,

Josef believed it was different for a woman to marry above her station. He couldn't imagine a man moving into the gentry through marriage. A restaurant owner or chef would never be acceptable to a titled lady. Therefore, he never said or did anything to show his feelings.

Occasionally, when they worked late, Josef and Anne would enjoy a glass of wine after the restaurant closed. Then, he'd drive her back to the cottage. She was completely settled there, and loved it. One night, when he took her home, Josef came very close to telling her how he felt, but backed out at the last minute. She wasn't even divorced yet, and it suddenly hit him that it would be highly improper to make any sort of romantic overture. Yet, he'd sensed that if he'd spoken, she wouldn't have been offended. In fact, she had rather encouraged him.

The moon was shining on a clear, starry night. Points of light in the sky caused the ocean water to twinkle as though it were scattered with diamonds. As the car pulled in front of the cottage, they'd been having a conversation about how much she loved living at the seaside. He turned off the engine, but left the radio playing. He began to tell her about his dream to someday build a house of his own, overlooking the water. He also told her that he hoped, at some point, to own another restaurant in the village. It wouldn't be the same sort as *Chez Chloe*, which was fine French cuisine, but more in the order of a French country Inn, with excellent, but more rural sorts of dishes, like Osso Buco, French crusted chicken pies, traditional onion soup and unique selections like Brie cheese croissants.

Anne thought his idea was wonderful. They chatted on, about how much they both loved the village and how nice the residents were. Finally, at one point, Anne asked a personal question.

"Josef, what kind of a woman are you looking for? I assume someday you'll want to marry. Please excuse me if I'm being too forward. I just feel we're close enough friends that I can ask that. Or, aren't you interested in marriage?"

Anne wasn't asking because she had any thoughts in her mind about herself. She didn't think she wanted any part of marriage, ever again. She was simply curious about her friend. Anyway, she was still in the midst of divorce proceedings.

"No, it's fine if you ask such a question. To tell the truth, I've never had time to give it much thought. My life has been rather chaotic. When we lived in Paris, my youth was spent at The Culinary Institute, training to be a chef. Then Elise and I moved to the country. The war came along, and afterwards I moved here. I've worked hard to start my business. Of course, I'd like to marry. I suppose I always thought I'd be married by now, but it just has never happened. There've been a few women who've interested me – very few, actually. Either the ones I wanted didn't want me, or I didn't want the ones who did want me," he laughed.

"I can't imagine why anyone wouldn't want you," she answered. "You're such a nice person – so decent and refined. Handsome, too," she smiled.

"Yes, well, it's the French, you know," he laughed, with an exaggerated shrug. "What about you, Anne? I've never wanted to bring up your marriage. I know it's a delicate subject. Are you ever going to be free of that scoundrel?"

"I hope so, Josef. He's so incredibly stubborn. He phoned my father last week and asked if Daddy would tell me to go back to him. Can you imagine?"

"Pardon me, but from what you've said, it's hard to imagine that he would think you'd want any part of him."

"That's certainly true. There's nothing on earth that would make me go back to him. I can't bear him. It's hard for me to believe I ever married him."

"Perhaps you didn't know him well enough," Josef answered.

"No, I didn't. It was a huge mistake. My one, big, regret in life." Anne laughed, and pointed to the sign outside of the car window. 'No Regrets'. Josef laughed, too. She sighed.

"All right – maybe one regret, but someday I'll be free of him. Then hopefully I'll regain my trust in men. But I intend to be very cautious, if there is a next time. It will be someone I know very, very well. I think it's better to be friends first, then lovers don't you think?"

A lovely song was playing on the car radio – one of the old songs from the war years. Josef's heart missed a beat.

"Yes, yes, I do. There is romance, and then there is love, you know. They are two very different things. Love takes time to grow. First there is friendship, then romance, then real love. I think that's the proper order."

There was silence in the car. He was twirling his fingers in and out of the steering column. She glanced over at him and, for a moment, wished she could slide across and put her arms around him. But she quickly caught herself. It was only the summer, the sea, and the night.

A commercial for a cleaning product suddenly blasted from the radio. The spell was broken. Josef got out of the car and walked around to open her door. Together they strolled up the pretty path leading to the cottage. He bent down and kissed her on the cheek, like a brother.

"Have a good night, Anne. Ring me tomorrow if you need anything."

18

The show was a week away. Everything was in place, except for Anne's coveted painting of her dogs. Anne thought about asking Alex to pick up the painting and bring it to Thornton-on-Sea, when she drove down for the show. But, Anne wasn't going to be able to attend the show, since she and her husband were going to be off on a two week trip to Switzerland. They were leaving that very afternoon. Anne was happy that Alex was getting some time off, and she never even mentioned the painting to her.

Her next thought was of Elise. Perhaps she should ask her to drive to London with her. But, that wasn't a good idea either, since she really had to have someone in the office to answer calls and inquiries about the show. Josef came to mind. She might ask him to accompany her. But, Josef had his own chores in order to be ready for the show. She finally decided that she was acting like a child. Frank wouldn't even be at St. Mary Abbott's Court. In all the time she'd known him, he had never once left the office to go home early. There was no reason on earth that he would do so now. Anne didn't need a security guard. Anyway, if she told anyone her plans, everyone would try to talk her out of going. She absolutely didn't want her parents to know, because she know they would worry themselves into a frenzy. She would make the trip, collect the painting, and be back in Thornton-on-Sea before anyone even missed her. Having decided what she was going to do, she decided to just be silent about it, and not start a big uproar.

She went back to work. A new client had rung that morning, wanting to set a time to talk with her. This one was a young bride, who wanted to schedule *Panache* to do a bridesmaid luncheon. It was another concept Anne had never done, but she thought it would be fun. She'd have to figure out who to use for models, since this was a bit different, and she couldn't see using the girls who would be in the wedding. After all, the show was being staged for them. She wasn't worried though. She knew from experience that an idea always presented itself.

Later that day, her longtime friend, the reporter from the *Times*, rang to make an appointment to interview and photograph her. They were going to run a large article about *Panache*, featuring Anne and Josef. Anne was delighted. She had been hoping for this. She'd sent a press release to the *Times*, but had no way of knowing whether they'd actually write anything. Apparently they thought it was newsworthy. There was no question it would help enormously. She rang Josef, giving him the time of the interview. He told her to ring him back when the reporter arrived. He thought it would be a good touch for the photos to be taken at the restaurant. Anne agreed.

Her busy day came to an end and Anne was more than ready to go home to her quaint cottage by the sea. On the way to her car, she ran into Elise Thornton. It was the first time they'd seen each other since the day they'd met at the cottage. Elise asked how Anne was getting along. She answered that everything was coming together wonderfully. Then Elise asked if she could stop by the office the next day to talk to Anne about part-time work.

Anne's mouth dropped open. "*You're* looking for part-time work? You? The Countess of Wexford, who is on every Board, and a member of every organisation in this village? Why would you want part-time work?" It was a rude question, but Anne was so surprised, she just blurted it out.

Elise laughed. "My dear, Anne. If I recall, you are Lady Anne Whitfield, the daughter of a Duke and Duchess. Why are you working?"

"Good point," Anne smiled. "But still, I'm not married, with children to look after." Elise and Sloan Thornton had welcomed a son into the world only recently. His name was Reese Rowan Thornton, and Anne knew Sloan must have been beside himself. He had the heir he'd longed for.

"I know, and I love my life. Everything is perfect. But I'd like to do something productive. I don't need the money, obviously. In fact, I'll donate my salary to a worthy cause. But I want to feel useful, beyond lending my name to charities and being a Mummy. Don't misunderstand, Anne. I'm potty over the children. The new baby is a gift from God. But we do have a nanny. I've spoken to Sloan about my feelings, and he's in full agreement. I don't even know if you'd want me. I just think your business is interesting, and I'd like to be a small part of it. I don't know what I could do – perhaps answer phones, type letters . . ."

"Elise. You would be a godsend. I need an assistant. How many hours a week did you have in mind?"

"Probably only three days. Perhaps more. Would that be sufficient?"

"Absolutely. I'd take whatever you're able to give me. I'm so surprised. You're the last person I thought I'd ever be lucky enough to have working as my assistant."

"Perhaps we should still sit down and talk about it. I feel rather awkward having stopped you on the street. You might want to think about it a bit more."

"No. I'm not about to give you a chance to change your mind. Come on. Let's go back to my office. We're only steps away. Do you have the time now?"

Elise looked at her wristwatch. "Yes, but only about half an hour. Will that do?"

"Yes, of course," Anne answered.

The two ladies walked back to *Panache*, and Anne unlocked the door. They went inside and sat down in the waiting area. "So, tell me what made you want a job," Anne asked.

"Just what I said outside. I'm very, very happy with my life. I have everything a woman could want, but I've always worked at something. To be honest, I get a little bored with going to meeting after meeting. I'm not really needed at half of them. Organisations just like to put my name on their stationery." They both laughed.

"Oh, I know all about that," Anne agreed. "I can understand why you'd want to have a real job."

"Yes. Your business is so fascinating to me. I love fashion, and the entire idea is appealing. I work well with people and would like to feel I'm worth more than just lending my name."

"You don't need to convince me. I'd love to have you. Of course I wish I could have you full time, but actually, at the moment I couldn't afford that anyway. We're still new, as you know, and I'm trying to be cautious about how money is spent. I know people think I'm so wealthy that money isn't an issue, but that's not true. I've taken a loan from my father to begin the business. But, I intend to pay him back, with interest. So I can't afford a very high wage."

"The salary doesn't matter a whit. As I said, I'll donate it to charity anyway. I suppose it's no different than volunteering, but for some reason I feel it's not the same."

"Elise, it's your business what you do with the money. Of course I want you. When would you be able to start?"

"I'd have to clear my calendar of a few obligations, but basically I think by the beginning of next week. Oh wait – don't you have a show next weekend? Perhaps I could help with that ahead of time?"

"I need someone to answer phones the Friday before the show. I have something rather important to do, that relates to the show. It will necessitate my being out of the office most of the day. If you could come in then, it would be perfect."

"I'll do a little better. Let's say I come in the day before, on Thursday. That will give you a chance to teach me the basics. Then I'll feel comfortable being left on my own, Friday."

"Elise, this is just terrific. Our meeting on the sidewalk must have been fate."

"That's funny. You know, Sloan has always believed our meeting each other was fate."

"Yes, I know," Anne answered. "Don't I know?" She laughed.

"Oh Anne, that was silly of me. I shouldn't have said that. It's so long ago, I'd almost forgotten."

"So have I, Elise. Actually, I'm glad Sloan met you for my own selfish reasons. If he hadn't, I wouldn't know you, and knowing you has turned out to be a very lucky thing for me."

"You're being too kind," Elise smiled. "But I feel the same way. I missed our friendship during the time we were estranged. I'm glad that's over."

"So am I. I think we'll make a good business team. You're perfect for this sort of venture.

"That's so nice, Anne. But I really don't want the job because of my looks. I'd like someone to think of me as more than a pretty face and an aristocratic name."

"I understand completely. And you're much more than that. I already know that from having taken French lessons from you. You're very intelligent. We're going to have a good time working together. I truly believe you'll help my business grow."

"Thanks so much, Anne." She looked at her watch again. "Well, I'd better run. I'll be here about eleven o'clock on Thursday. Will that work? I thought I might work from eleven to three o'clock. That way I'll be home when Chloe gets back from her school."

"Perfect. You've solved a big problem for me. I'll look forward to seeing you on Thursday, then."

They both stood and gathered their belongings. As they left the office, Anne impulsively hugged Elise. "Thanks so much for telling me you wanted to work. I wouldn't have dreamed of asking you."

"I'm awfully glad I did. Until Thursday," Elise smiled.

"I'll see you then," said Anne. They both walked in separate directions to their cars.

19

The week flew by. On Thursday, Elise was very prompt. Anne loved having someone else in the office. Elise showed poise and grace as she fielded telephone calls. She had a nice way of working with others, never losing her patience and speaking in that sweet voice which made people instantly feel close to her.

Anne was more than ready to head for London on Friday, knowing *Panache* was in capable hands. She'd explained again to Elise about the necessity for her absence, and emphasized that if anyone needed her, she should take a note, and Anne get back to them as soon as she returned. Elise was to use her own superb judgment to handle any problems that arose, and when in doubt, ask Josef.

She left Thornton-on-Sea right after Elise came into the office. It was a lovely, late summer day. She'd dressed casually, in a pretty flowered dress and brushed her hair into a top knot. She looked like a young girl, and no one would have believed she was nearing thirty. She felt good about what she'd accomplished in the past few months and only wished Frank would stop acting like a fool. She wanted him gone from her life permanently. She was living as though she was unattached when, in reality, she was still married. Anne believed that he had to come to his senses soon. She'd almost reached the point where she would agree to let him have the house, just so he was firmly finally behind her. But it made her furious to think about such a thing. The fact that he would receive half of the selling price was enough to send her into orbit. He already had the money from her dowry. You'd think that would have satisfied him. But, Anne knew money wasn't the real reason for his obstinate behaviour. He enjoyed being able to control her, by not agreeing to a settlement. When she thought back, she realised how controlling he'd been. It was the dominant feature in his personality. She truly wanted to kick herself for having been such a fool. She'd learned an enormous lesson from the awful fiasco. Never again would she act so impulsively when it came to a life-altering decision.

The drive to London didn't seem overly long, and before she knew it, she was bumper to bumper in congested traffic. It didn't concern Anne. She was a good driver and had a lot of patience. She simply let her mind wander while sitting behind other cars. The only thing that mattered was collecting the painting, and leaving before Frank came home. He never arrived until at least six o'clock. She hoped to be back in Thornton-on-Sea by then

She watched people on the sidewalks. When a young mother passed, pushing a pram, her heart ached for a moment. If everything had turned out well, she too would be pushing a pram. She tried to shake off the feeling of sadness, by thinking about the sort of father Frank would have made. For the first time, she had to admit that losing the baby had probably been a blessing. The child would have had a miserable existence. Anne had no doubt that Frank would have used a son or daughter in the same way he was using the house – as a means to keep her tied to him. The child's feelings wouldn't have mattered. Again, she was angry with herself for not having prosecuted him. Perhaps, if she had done so, it would have kept him from creating havoc in some other poor woman's life. Anne had no doubt that he'd remarry eventually, if for no other reason than the need for someone to press his trousers.

⟶ ⁓ ⟵

She pulled into the gravelled drive at St. Mary Abbott's Court at a little after twelve o'clock. Everything was quiet. She stepped out of the car and walked up the path to the front door. Suddenly the thought struck that Frank might have had the locks changed. He'd have had no right to do such a thing, since the place was as much hers as his, but it wouldn't have been out of the question. However, when she put her key into the lock, it turned smoothly. Anne heaved a sigh of relief. The door opened, and she entered the house for the first time since leaving by ambulance in February.

Everything was neat. At least he was taking proper care of it. She didn't loiter, heading straight to the small room where her painting of the three cherished pets was hanging. It wasn't surprising that it had been missed when the movers came. Still recuperating in hospital, Anne hadn't been there to supervise.

The room in question wasn't very large. None of the furniture in it had been Anne's. Everything had come from Frank's flat in Nottinghill. It held an old leather sofa and two chairs, along with the desk he'd had at university. There was a much nicer room that served as an office on the first level, so this one had scarcely been used. The painting of the dogs hung above the desk. She gingerly removed it from the wall. Anne wrapped the frame with a large blanket she'd brought. It would have to go into the backseat of her car, since it was too large for the boot. She didn't want it to get torn, or marred in any way. Unrolling a long piece of sturdy twine from a supply she'd also brought, Anne wound it over the blanket, and tied it, to be certain it was secure. Then she picked it up and began to move toward the entrance. The painting was heavier than she'd remembered. She had to stop several times to rest. The hallway leading to the entrance was quite lengthy, requiring that she go down one stretch and make a left turn to the foyer. Just as she was about to do so, she heard the front door open. Her heart almost stopped. Who in the world could be coming into the house unannounced? Did Frank have someone keeping watch during the day? Perhaps it was only a neighbour. She propped the painting against the wall and rounded the corner. Frank stood there, with an expectant look on his face.

"So. You've decided to come back to me, have you? I wondered how much longer it would take before you came to your senses. I was very happy when I got the call from Brian. He saw your car pull into the driveway and rang me immediately. Did you forget that Brian and I are chums?"

Brian Garner was a neighbour. He was married and had two small children. He and Frank had met when they'd moved in, and the two had become friendly, attending soccer games and occasionally meeting at the local pub for a pint on Saturday afternoons. Yes, Anne had forgotten about Brian, primarily because Brian also worked in London. She'd never dreamed he'd be home on a weekday. Her face must have looked puzzled, because Frank went on to say that fortunately Brian had taken a few days leave from work to oversee some remodeling being done at his house.

"If you've decided to come back to me, why didn't you ring? I'd have made certain I was here to greet you. I'm so glad to see you, Anne. I knew that sooner or later we'd get beyond this spat."

Anne was astounded. "Spat? You call what happened between us a spat? My God, Frank. Because of what you did, I lost a baby and landed in hospital. I might have had you arrested for assault. That wasn't a spat."

"Why are you bringing all of that up again? We've talked about it until it's been run into the ground. That's all in the past, and we need to be looking to the future."

"Are you daft? Nothing in the world could induce me to come back to you. Nothing. I thought you understood that by now. I'm not here to argue. I had no idea I'd see you. I drove up to collect a painting that was overlooked when my things were moved. I need it for a fashion show that I'm coordinating tomorrow night."

"A fashion show? Where? In that pathetic, little, village where your parents live? I can't believe you're serious, Anne."

"Well, I *am* serious. I've started my own business, and it's flooded with clients. It's going to be a huge success. I'm not living with my parents anymore. I have my own cottage. In short, I've moved on with my life, Frank. I decided not to let you ruin my entire future. You're nothing to me, Frank. Nothing. If you'd stop the foolishness about a settlement, you could get on with your life, too."

"I don't believe you, Anne. I think you're using the excuse of a fool painting to see me again. I know you still love me. We're married. You can't just brush that off so easily. I took the vows we made seriously."

"Yes, of course you did, Frank. The way you acted when you were told I was expecting a baby proves how seriously you took them. It's too bad there was nothing in the marriage vows about putting the desire for a yacht, a country house and a tour of the continent ahead of a child."

Frank ran his hand through his hair. "Go up to the nursery. I've been working like a fool on a baby cot. I'm completely ready to try for another child. I've even decided to postpone thoughts of those things you mentioned, until after we have a baby. You see? Everything will be the way you want."

"Frank. I am not coming back to you. Get that through your head. Nothing could make me do that. I don't love you. I don't think I ever loved you. What's more, I don't believe you ever loved me. You said as much when you blurted out that you didn't think you'd have to support me, let alone a baby."

"Oh for God's sake. I said something you didn't like. So that's a reason to end a marriage? You're very shallow, Anne."

Anne turned around and took hold of the painting. Then, she began to carry it toward the door. Frank was standing directly in front of her.

"Please move, Frank. I need to get this to my car. I'm due back in Thornton-on-Sea in a little over an hour."

His face took on the thunderous look she knew so well.

"You aren't going anywhere. I've had enough of your foolishness. You're staying right here, where you belong. We're going to reconcile, and I'm not putting up with any more of your stupid arguments. You've been acting like a spoiled brat. One little fight, and you run home to your parents. Marriage is a commitment, Anne. Do you remember promising 'for better or for worse'?"

Anne was growing frightened. After all, this horrid man had once beaten her until she was unconscious. She knew what he was capable of. She decided to take a different approach.

"All right, Frank. Yes, I do remember. I'm sorry I've been so stubborn. But please, help me get this painting to my car, because I really do have to take it back to Thornton-on-Sea. It's the centrepiece of a show that will be staged tomorrow night. After that, I'll return to London, and we'll talk."

"I repeat, Anne. You're not going anywhere. It's time you were taught a lesson. Do you think you can just play around with a man's feelings? Just because you have a posh title? You think you don't need me for anything, but you aren't going to get away with this. I'm your husband. You'll obey me. Do you understand?"

Anne didn't know what to do. He might do anything to her. She needed to get away from him. She thought for a moment. If she could only get to the car, all she'd need was a short head- start. She could lock the doors, drive away and never see him again. If he followed, she'd drive to the nearest police station. She should never have come to London, alone.

"All right, Frank. You're right. I'll obey you, but please let me get this painting into the car. Even if I'm not at the show tomorrow, the painting has to be there. I'll ring Alex, and ask her to drive it down there. She was coming to the show anyway. She can take the train back from Thornton-on-Sea."

"Quit lying, Anne. Alex isn't coming to your show. Did you forget that as Personnel Director, I'm the person who signs off on all vacations? As we speak, Alex is in Switzerland"

"Oh. Yes. I totally forgot that. Well, that won't do at all then, will it. Nonetheless, let's get it to the car and I'll find someone else from London who will drive it to Kent for me.

Frank looked wary, but Anne could tell he was wavering. There was silence for several moments. Finally he spoke.

"Fine. I'll carry it out to the car. You stay inside. Stand right here, in the open door, so I can keep an eye on you. Where do you want it? It will probably have to go into the backseat. It looks too large for the boot."

"Damn," thought Anne. "Damn. Now what?" She couldn't argue about being the one to carry it. The only thing she could do was try to make a run for it while he was carrying the painting to the car. She'd parked to the right side of the house. There was no way he could keep her in his sight the entire time. She would have to give it a go. It was the only hope she had.

"All right. That will be fine," she answered. Frank walked over and took hold of the painting. He was much stronger than she was. He picked it up with ease.

"Follow me, and when I open the door, stand right in the centre. Don't move."

"I won't," she answered.

Frank opened the door and stepped across the threshold. He was holding the painting above the ground. He carried it down the three steps and turned in the direction of the car. His back was to Anne, but he stopped every few steps, keeping watch behind him. He'd moved about half way, when Anne decided it was then or never. She began to run as swiftly as she possibly could. Unfortunately, she'd worn high heels. They were kicked off, so she could move more quickly. Her aim was to make it to a neighbour's home and scream bloody murder until someone heard her and came to help. She'd reached the end of the drive. There was a house to the left. She knew the owners. They were aware of what had taken place when she'd ended up in hospital. She knew they wouldn't hesitate to help. But she only managed a few more steps before she felt Frank's arms grab her from behind. Anne went down in a heap. Before she could start to scream, he put one hand over her mouth and began to drag her back to the house. She was utterly helpless. Looking around frantically, it was obvious that nothing was happening in any of the nearby homes. The neighbourhood was completely still. Frank got her up the steps and pushed her into the foyer. She lay on the floor sobbing.

He slammed the front floor, yanking Anne to her feet. Shoving her up against the wall, he began to yell.

"I knew I couldn't trust you. You think you're so bloody smart. You think because you're a hoity-toity aristocrat that I'm not good enough for you."

He slapped her viciously across the face. The force of the blow caused a cut on her lower lip. Blood began to seep down her chin.

"Please stop, Frank. Think what you're doing. Do you want to end up in prison? You'll lose your job, and everything you've worked hard for all of your life." Anne was crying hysterically. She hoped her words would get through, but they had the opposite effect.

"You think you have the right to take away everything in my life? Well, you're dead wrong. You won't be going to the authorities. I'll teach you a lesson you won't ever forget."

He hit her again. This time his fist landed on her cheek, and she felt bones crush. He picked her up and began to carry her up the stairway, while her small fists beat against him. She was in terrible pain. He laughed at her feeble attempts. Once they reached the top of the stairs, Frank took her into one of the guest rooms, throwing her onto the bed. "Oh God," thought Anne. 'He's going to rape me." But she was wrong. He took off his tie and tightly bound her hands. Then, he reached behind him, into a dresser drawer, and found a woolen winter scarf she'd given him. He used that to bind her legs at the ankles. Anne thought she might be able to get loose from the items he'd used. The fabric in each would likely tear. However, it turned out that those articles were only temporary. He had no intention of leaving her permanently bound with a tie and a scarf. He doubled up his fist and hit her again on the side of her head. She momentarily blacked out.

"If you want me to stop hitting you, then you'd better not move. Stay there and be still. I'm going to walk across the room to my desk in the sitting area. If you make one move, so help me, I'll kill you."

Anne knew he meant it. He was completely off his head. The worst thing she could have done was to blurt out the warning she'd given about ruining his life with his actions. It had totally unhinged him. She lay still as a mouse, trying to stop weeping. What was going to happen to her? There was no expectation of help until God only knew how long. No one would be concerned about her until she failed to return to Thornton-on-Sea, and then they'd probably wait to see if she'd been detained in traffic, or had car trouble. No one knew where she had gone. They wouldn't really become frantic until a few hours before the show, when she still hadn't arrived. By the time help arrived, she could well be dead.

Frank returned to the bed, with a ball of heavy twine – the kind you used to tie heavy parcels. He had scissors and wide masking tape. Tying her arms and feet with the heavy cord, he covered that with the tape. She couldn't move her feet or her legs at all. Lastly, he placed several pieces of tape across her mouth. When he was finished, he picked her up, like a human bundle, and carried her up the stairs to the next level. There was a box room up there. It was filled with luggage and cartons full of items like Christmas decorations. He cleared a space and dumped her in it. Then, he covered all trace of her with the articles he'd taken out to make room. She was unable to move, or make a sound. Switching out the light, he slammed the door.

She could hear his footsteps descending the staircase. There was no longer the slightest bit of hope that she was going to get away from him. He was going to torture her and let her die a slow, agonizing death. She was too frightened to cry. It would have been virtually impossible anyway, since her mouth was covered, and she could only breathe through her nose. If she began to sob, her nose would be useless, and she'd suffocate. Anne tried to concentrate on taking in air through her nostrils, while ignoring the searing pain she felt from blows he'd delivered. She closed her eyes, counting her heartbeats. If she could calm down, perhaps she would fall asleep. She prayed he wouldn't return and do anything worse. Starving to death or dying of dehydration were preferable to being beaten to a pulp, but neither was very attractive.

She wondered what time it was. She tried to estimate how many hours had passed since her arrival. The blow to her head, combined with fright and anxiety, made her unable to think clearly. It was probably about three o'clock. No one would expect her back in Thornton-on-Sea yet. Finally shock took over and numbed her pain. Anne fell asleep, with her head resting on a suitcase.

20

She awoke to complete silence. She was terribly thirsty, and her head was pounding with pain. Her entire face felt like it was swollen to twice its normal size. She needed a toilet. Anne had no idea how much time had passed. It was pitch dark in the box room, and there were no windows, so she was completely disoriented. Lying with her head still on the suitcase, she tried to come to grips with the terrifying nightmare she was undergoing.

After what seemed an eternity, there were footsteps. The door opened, and Frank was standing in front of her, holding a sandwich and a glass of water. The light in the hallway was on, and she blinked rapidly. It was the first bit of illumination she'd been exposed to since the door had been closed. It took her eyes a moment to adjust.

"Well, good morning, Anne. Did you have a good rest?" Frank asked, as though she'd just awoken in their pretty bed.

She simply stared at him. What else could she have done, since her mouth was still taped shut? Frank was speaking in a friendly voice. He was acting like there was nothing untoward about the situation.

"You know, Anne, I would be happy to let you have a bite to eat and a drink of water. I imagine you'd also like to visit the loo."

She nodded her head vigorously.

"None of this would have been necessary, if you'd agreed to come home and had stopped acting like a child. It isn't too late, you know. We can still be happy. But I don't have a lot of trust in you anymore. I'm afraid you'_ have to think of some way to show me that you still love me. Would you like to have something to eat and drink?"

Again, Anne nodded her head. Tears began to stream down her face.

"There's no need to cry. Here, I'll untie your legs, and remove the tape from your mouth. For the time being, I'm going to leave your hands bound. But if you re-earn some of my trust, perhaps I'll not retie you and will even let your hands go free."

He did as he'd promised. Anne was overjoyed at being able to get some circulation back into her legs. Also, it was heaven to take a full breath of air. She winced when she opened her mouth. The split lip was still an open wound. Blood had crusted over it. Her feet and calves were numb, but there was the beginning of tingling as feeling began to return. Anne was afraid to speak, for fear she'd upset him in some way, and he'd bind her again. Still, she absolutely had to use the bathroom, so she took a chance, asking his permission.

"Yes. I'll walk there with you. I'm afraid I can't close the door, because you've acted so dreadfully. I'm going to have to watch your every move. Come, I'll help you stand."

He reached his hands out, putting them round her waist. Since her hands were still tied tightly, it was difficult to find her balance. Finally she stood, wobbling back and forth. He took hold of her arm, and they shuffled down the hallway to the master bedroom. Then they turned into the doorway, and guided her to the toilet. He allowed her to enter and use the facilities, but watched the entire time. Anne was past the point of embarrassment. That was the least of her concerns. When finished, he took a cloth, washed her hands, and dried them. Then he led her back to the box room. She'd been able to see the windows in the bedroom and could tell that it was definitely morning. It was probably about nine o'clock, though it could have been later.

Once back in the box room, Frank let her have the sandwich. Since her hands were useless, he fed it to her in small bites. In between, he offered sips of water. She wished she could grab the glass and gulp it all down. Still, the awful dryness in her mouth dissipated.

"Do you think you could behave, if I untied your hands?" he asked.

"Yes. I'll be good," she murmured.

"All right. Let's give it a go."

He deftly took the twine and tape off. Anne flexed her hands and fingers. They were as numb as her legs had been. She sat on the floor, head hung low, still weeping. There was silence again.

"Anne. You've been awfully foolish. I can't for the life of me think why you've acted like this. You've kept me in a constant state of anxiety, since all of this began. Now, if you're ready to prove to me that you're sorry and that you want us to be happy like we once were, I'm ready to forgive you. I *do* still love you, you know. I've wanted to feel your body next to mine for so long. Are you ready to give me the pleasure you once did?"

Anne felt sick to her stomach. She couldn't imagine letting him touch her intimately. Yet, what else could she do? She was absolutely certain he was completely insane. If she didn't acquiesce, God only knew what would come next.

She looked up at him and nodded her head.

"Tell me you love me, Anne."

"I love you, Frank," she answered.

"Let's go into the bedroom, shall we? Unfortunately, your pretty nightwear is no longer here, so I'll have to forgo the pleasure of watching you undress and slip into something whimsical. You'll need to have everything brought back. What an awful inconvenience, Anne."

She faithfully followed him to the bedroom. Try as she might, she couldn't stop weeping. Once they were on the bed, she spoke.

"Frank, could I please just have a few moments to relax. I don't feel very well, after last night. My head hurts, and my mouth is dreadfully sore. So is my cheek. I think some bones were broken."

"I'm sorry about that, Anne, but it was necessary. I hope you're not going to make me lose trust in you again. I really don't want to injure you anymore."

"No. Don't lose trust in me, please. I'm still just a bit shaky. I don't want to disappoint you. If you'll only wait a bit, I'm sure I'll be fine."

"I can't wait, Anne. I've been waiting for months now. I'll let you go into the bathroom. Wash your face. Perhaps a warm cloth will make your bruises feel better. You can also take some aspirin for your headache. It's still in the cabinet, where we've always kept it."

Anne crawled stiffly off the bed, making her way slowly to the toilet. Upon reaching the doorway, she turned and asked if he would mind if she took a bath.

"I would feel so much better. I know you'd rather I be clean and fresh for you."

"Yes, I suppose that would be acceptable. But don't linger."

"Must I keep the door open again?"

"No. I'm going to trust that you won't do anything foolish. We're going to pretend like this is our wedding night again, and everything else is in the past. I'll be anxiously waiting for you, darling."

Anne entered the bathroom, closing the door. She wanted to lock it, but sensed such a move might set Frank off again. She started to run water in the tub. Walking to the sink, she looked into the mirror. She was horrified. The entire right side of her face was swollen, at least twice its normal size. Her cheek was horribly bruised, and she could see that bones had been broken. There was an enormous bruise where he'd hit her above the ear, and her eye was swollen. Her mouth looked like she'd been in a prizefight. The bottom lip was distorted, crusted with dried blood. An open wound ran from the inside of her mouth to her chin. On top of that, a tooth had been knocked loose.

"Oh my God," she mouthed quietly. "I'll never be the same again." She couldn't stop the tears. How could she walk back into that bedroom and let such a monster touch her? Yet, how could she not? Continuing to run the tub, Anne turned to the faucet in the sink. Taking a cloth, she gently washed her face. The soap stung when it touched her mouth, and she could scarcely stand to put pressure on her cheek. Still, she knew it had to be done to prevent infection.

After that, she put some toothpaste in her mouth, rubbing it on her teeth with a finger. Then she turned back toward the tub. Turning off the faucet, she stepped into the soothing water. It felt so good. Lying back in the tub, she tried to relax, but it simply wasn't possible. Anne didn't think she had the wherewithal to go back into the bedroom. There was a window in the bath, overlooking the yard and a neighbour's house beyond the lawn. Did she have the courage to open it and shout? She thought about it, but discarded the idea. Even if someone heard her, there was no way they could reach her in time. Frank was a big man, perfectly capable of breaking down the door if she locked it. She was totally helpless.

Stepping out of the tub, Anne sank to her knees on the bare tile. She began to pray. There was nothing left to do. She was reciting a litany in her mind, of every prayer she'd ever learned; The Lord's Prayer; The Twenty-Third Psalm; prayers said at bedtime when she was a child. She sobbed harder when she remembered the words 'If I should die before I wake, I pray the Lord my soul to take.'

Suddenly the door opened, and Frank burst into the room.

"What the bloody hell are you doing on your knees, like you're in a church? I let you come in here to bathe, not to pray. If you want to thank God for placing forgiveness in my heart, then you can do that after we've made love. Now come, Anne. I'm tired of waiting."

Anne stayed on her knees and began to wail.

"I can't do it, Frank. I just can't. I'm hurt. I need medical attention. Can't you see how terribly injured I am?"

He grabbed her. Pulling her to her feet, he slapped her across the wounded cheek. The pain was excruciating.

"I told you what you're going to do. I don't bloody care how hurt you are. You brought it on yourself."

"No," she shouted. "No. You're a monster. I can't go through any more."

Anne was hysterical. Somewhere in the recesses of her mind she knew she was probably signing her death warrant, but she wasn't going to give in to him like a sheep.

Frank made a fist, hitting her in the nose. Once again, she heard bone crunch. Blood was dripping down her face. He was doubling up to hit her again, when there was a noise. He swung his head around. There, in the doorway, stood Josef! Was it a mirage? Was she so totally defeated that she was hallucinating? Or had God answered her prayers?

He was definitely real. Josef grabbed Frank by the collar and dragged him into the bedroom. He slammed him up against the wall, and bashed his fist into Frank's jaw. Frank immediately collapsed onto the floor. The strong man, who'd been doing such a fine job of beating a woman half his size, couldn't defend himself against one punch from another man. He started to struggle to his feet, but Josef warned him to stay where he was.

"I'd love an excuse to break your neck. Stay put," Josef shouted.

Then, of all people, Elise came into the room. Of course, she was Josef's sister, but Elise was such a gentle creature, it was hard to imagine her in such a violent setting. Anne stumbled out of the bathroom just in time to see her arrive. When she spotted Anne, she pulled a blanket from a chair, wrapped it around her and led her to the bed.

"Lie down, dear heart. Josef is calling the authorities. It's all over now. Frank will be put where he can never hurt anyone again."

"Elise. How did you get here? I'm so glad to see you. I'm not very clear in my mind. Forgive me if I seem a bit jumbled."

Josef walked to the telephone and called Scotland Yard. Anne heard him say there'd been a terrible assault, and he needed both police detectives and an ambulance. After he hung up, he sat down next to Anne. She was trembling, from a combination of relief and pain. Josef reached down and embraced her gently.

"Anne. Oh my dearest, Anne. How could anyone do something so evil to you?"

He rocked her in his arms. Elise continued to murmur kind words, as well. Frank huddled in the corner afraid to stand, knowing Josef would come after him again if he moved. Anne looked up at Josef, sobbing and clutching the fabric of his jacket.

"Josef. Josef. You saved my life. Truly, you did. He would have killed me. I prayed to God that I'd be saved, and there you were. I can't believe you're here. How did you know where to find me?"

"Nobody knew you weren't back until this morning. When you weren't in Thornton-on-Sea when it was time to close the office, Elise locked up, and came over to Chez Chloe to tell me that you'd had to do something important, and might not be back until early evening. I assumed it had something to do with the show, and didn't pay it much mind. We all went home for the night. But, when you still hadn't returned this morning, we became very concerned. I drove over to the cottage, but your car was gone.

Then, I rang Elise, and she couldn't imagine where you might be. But, she did remember that you mentioned having to pick up a painting of dogs for the show. We hated to ring your parents. It was perfectly obvious that you'd made the decision to drive to London and collect the painting on your own. That's when we became worried. We had no idea what was going on. We were afraid to ring the house, in case Frank was here. For the same reason, we were afraid to call the authorities. If they'd shown up, it might have made things worse. Of course, now it's evident that it couldn't have been much worse. Anyway, Elise and I jumped into the car, and drove as fast as possible to London. It's clear that we arrived just in the nick of time. Why didn't you tell me you were coming here to London? I never would have let you make the trip without me. I should have spoken up before – should have made you promise never to do anything silly, like agreeing to see that disgusting man you married. I knew something like this would happen, if you ever allowed yourself to be alone with him. But, I was more frightened of speaking up and telling you my honest feelings. I love you, Anne. I love you with all of my heart."

Anne closed her eyes. Was she dreaming? Perhaps she'd already died. She opened them again. Josef was still there. Still holding her. Still murmuring that he loved her. She was anything but dead. In spite of the pain she felt, her heart was racing with happiness. How could she not have recognised that she loved him, too?

"I'm sorry, Josef. I never should have come to London alone. I didn't think Frank would be here. I've caused you all to worry so, and I've ruined the show tonight."

"No, sweet Anne. You've ruined nothing. Elise will go ahead with the show. You're going straight to hospital. I'll let my assistant chef handle the dinner. I'm staying with you. He bent down, and kissed her gently. "Oh Anne, I do love you so."

"You were right," Anne whispered.

"What was I right about, Anne?"

"You were right when you said first comes friendship, then romance, then love."

"I think we missed most of the romance," he answered softly.

"No. We're in that phase right now. It's going to last a long time."

Josef softly touched her swollen lips with his.

"Yes, *Mon Cherie*. A long, long time."

AFTERWORD

Anne Whitfield Lisak sat in the first row, relishing the applause, as members of the Animal Aid Society strutted down the runway, modeling the latest in autumn fashions. It was the second annual show for that organization, and it was packed with people who'd enjoyed a wonderful dining experience at her husband's restaurant. Anne looked lovely. Months of recuperation and surgery had paid off. The awful damage done by Frank DeLuca's vicious cruelty was a thing of the past. Frank himself sat in a psychiatric hospital for the criminally insane, and it would be a long time, if ever, before he would be released.

Elise and Sloan Thornton, with their two children, Chloe and Reese, sat next to Anne and Josef. Who would ever have believed that Anne would end up as Sloan's sister-in-law? She and Josef, married six months, had just moved into the beautiful home they'd built. It was on a stretch of land near the old cottage, where the sign still read 'No Regrets'. They'd purchased the land from Sloan and Elise. Instead of tearing down the cottage, they'd decided to keep it and construct a dream house nearby. It was now a showplace in Thornton-on-Sea. The two couples would still share use of the cottage as a guesthouse.

Anne's business was flourishing, and Elise Thornton had become her full partner. They made a wonderful team, never seeming to tire of each other's company, in spite of the fact that they were also sisters-in-law. Anne had earned enough profit to pay back her father for his generous loan to start *Panache*. She and Elise had completely redecorated the office to reflect their love of fashion. It also reflected their love of animals. Behind the reception, desk hung the irreplaceable painting of three beloved terriers, sitting on a sofa. In addition, each woman had two little puppies at home, adopted from the same, shelter litter. Anne's parents weren't present for the show. Lady Caroline was busy tending to their new baby boy, Adrian Bennett Whitfield, Jr., the new heir to Meadowlands.

Life was a strange thing. Anne had once been positive that Sloan was the only man she could ever love. It had taken a series of bad choices for Anne to realise, just as Sloan had, that she should have trusted God to send her soulmate into her life. Her prayers had been answered. Josef was the one fate had in store. Anne had embraced many truths in the past year. Perhaps the most important was that it wasn't always evident whether a man was a gentleman by the way he dressed, his education, occupation, or manner of speaking.

OTHER BOOKS BY MARY CHRISTIAN PAYNE

The Somerville Trilogy

Willow Grove Abbey: Book 1 of the Somerville Trilogy
St. James Road: Book 2 of the Somerville Trilogy
Serendipity: Book 3 of the Somerville Trilogy

The Claybourne Trilogy

The White Feather: Book 1 of the Claybourne Trilogy
The White Butterfly: Book 2 of the Claybourne Trilogy
White Cliffs of Dover: Book 3 of the Claybourne Trilogy

The Thornton Trilogy

No Regrets: Book 1 of The Thornton Trilogy
No Gentleman: Book 2 of the Thornton Trilogy
No Secrets: Book 3 of the Thornton Trilogy

ABOUT THE AUTHOR

Mary Christian Payne was highly successful in several management positions in Fortune 500 Companies, in New York City, St. Louis, Missouri, Orlando Florida, and Tulsa, Oklahoma. Her work included Grant writing, and designing and writing Training Manuals for Executive Training Programs.

She left the corporate world, and became Director of Career Development at the Women' Resource Center at the University of Tulsa, where she designed a program that enabled hundreds of adult women to return to college and better their lives. She received the Mayor's Pinnacle Award in 1993 for this achievement. Mary left that position when the Center closed, and then opened her own Career Counseling Center. She retired in 2008.

Mary Christian Payne became a successful, best-selling author at the age of 71, with the help of her publisher, Tom Corson-Knowles. All of her life, she had wanted to write, and had received accolades for her unpublished work. She was encouraged in college, and writing was a significant part of the various jobs she held.

In 2013, she read Tom Corson-Knowles' book about publishing on Kindle. She wrote to him and he telephoned her. The rest is history. Since that time, she has published nine books, with more on the way.

Mary lost her husband in June, 2015, after 33 years of marriage. The grief process brought a lull to her writing, but she found that putting words on paper helped immensely. She is now in the process of writing her second novel since his death. She lives in Tulsa, Oklahoma, with her two beloved Maltese dogs.

Sign up for the newsletter to get news, updates and new release info from Mary Christian Payne:

http://bit.ly/MaryChristianPayne

One Last Thing...

If you enjoyed this book, I'd be very grateful if you'd post a short review on Amazon. Your support really does make a difference and I read all the reviews personally.

Thanks again for your support!